THE PLACE
CALLED
QUIRPON
(Kar-poon)

EARL B. PILGRIM

DRC PUBLISHING
3 Parliament Street
St. John's, Newfoundland and Labrador
A1A 2Y6
Telephone: (709) 726-0960
E-mail: staceypj@nl.rogers.com
www.drcpublishingnl.com

Library and Archives Canada Cataloguing in Publication

Pilgrim, Earl B. (Earl Baxter), 1939-
    The place called Quirpon / Earl B. Pilgrim.

ISBN 978-1-926689-39-5

    1. Dewar, Neil, b. 1793--Fiction. 2. Rebecca (Schooner)--Fiction.
3. Shipwrecks--Newfoundland and Labrador--Fiction. I. Title.

PS8581.I338P53 2011   C813'.54   C2011-903496-4

Layout and design by Becky Pendergast
Cover sketch by Earl B. Pilgrim
Cover sketch colorized by Glynn McDonald

Published 2011
Printed in Canada

We acknowledge the financial support of the Government of Canada through the
Canada Book Fund (CBF) for our publishing activities.

Table of Contents

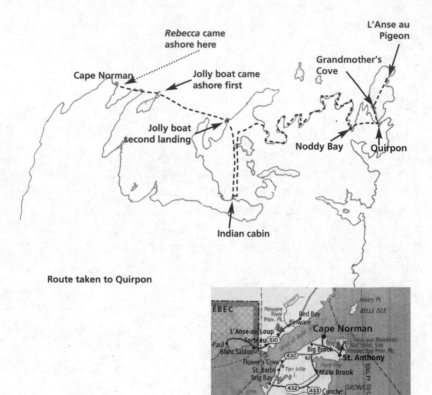

Rebecca came ashore here

L'Anse au Pigeon

Grandmother's Cove

Cape Norman

Jolly boat came ashore first

Jolly boat second landing

Noddy Bay

Quirpon

Indian cabin

Route taken to Quirpon

Dedication

This book is dedicated to my brother, Junior Murray Canning, who passed away on February 12, 2011, at age 65.

Junior taken at L'Anse au Pigeon

Junior was anxious to see the finished product, but that was something that was not to be. The book was not completed until after his death. I was asked by Memorial University to consider writing a book about Neil Dewar, the young Scottish-born sailor who lost his arms and legs after his ship *Rebecca* was wrecked off Cape Norman on the Northern Peninsula on November 20, 1816. It was Isaac Isaacs, an Englishman based in Quirpon, who was responsible for saving Neil's life. The young man, whose story is well known to people on the Northern Peninsula, told of his terrible ordeal in a work entitled Narrative of the Shipwreck and Suffering of Neil Dewar. After I studied the narrative I gave it to my brother, Junior, and he agreed a story about the incident should be written. As I wrote, Junior read what I was doing and offered suggestions at every turn of the road as Neil and his companions trudged onward. I had reached almost the end of *The Place Called Quirpon* when Junior passed away after a long battle with cancer.

Earl B. Pilgrim

Chapter 1

JOINING THE NAVY

The day was long for a twelve-year-old boy scrubbing rust off sheets of steel in the blazing sun. In the boy's mind, what he was doing was pure murder, next to slavery.

Young Neil Dewar was the son of Simon Dewar, who felt it was in both of their best interests to introduce the boy to the wheel and axel trade in the company owned by Mr. Joseph McNeill. Simon had worked as a wheelwright for the company for twenty years.

"If you learn the trade, son, you will always have a job," he was fond of telling Neil. "You have to start early in life just like I did and work your way up."

But young Neil was fed up with scrubbing rust off iron buggy shoes with a steel brush in the boiling sun. He would rather do anything else on earth. He hated the work and told his father so.

Neil started school at age seven and quickly moved up in his grades. He was a clever lad and always at the top of his class. One of his favourite teachers was an ex-naval officer everyone called the Admiral.

The Admiral told many a tale of the sea to the boys in his classes. The Admiral also told Simon Dewar that young Neil had the potential of becoming a naval officer some day. He said Simon should try to influence his son to aim for a naval career.

But Simon Dewar vowed his son would never go to sea. He was not impressed with the idea of a naval career. Simon had seen too much of the Royal Navy. Men taken by press gangs and forced into service on naval ships. Men terrorized into doing their duty. Men half starved and miserable. Men pushed around in the name of the King without being paid. That was no life for his son.

"No sir, Neil will never be a sailor," he would tell his wife Maggie.

Simon and Maggie were living in Lochgilphead, Argyleshire, Scotland, when Neil was born in 1793. When Simon had finished his apprenticeship in the steel manufacturing business, he got a job with the McNeill Steel Works and moved his family from Scotland to Oakfield, on the Isle of Wight in the south of England. Neil was two years old at the time.

Simon Dewar was a burly man who could fit in anywhere. He was good humoured, well liked, and a hard worker. He was also a good family man. When he wasn't working, he spent all of his time with his family.

Young Neil had his father's broad shoulders and big hands. He followed in his father's footsteps, all the way to the age of twelve when he started working in the iron-steel yard during the summers, cleaning rust off sheets of iron with a steel brush.

Neil didn't complain to the other boys who endured the heat and flies with him. He kept his thoughts to himself so as not to influence them. But, as the summer months of torture moved along, Neil vowed he would not spend the rest of his life surrounded by iron.

"When I become a man, I will never go near a sheet of iron or steel again," he told his mother one day.

"I can't blame anyone being fed up doing such work," she said with a sigh.

After telling his father he hated the work, Neil didn't complain to him again. It wasn't good for boys of his age to complain. It was grin and bear it and hope to be alive and well when school opened again after the summer recess.

In school, the Admiral spent a lot of time teaching geography and military history. The battle of Trafalgar and Admiral Nelson was his speciality. Neil and the other boys were enthralled by the story of twenty-seven ships led by Admiral Lord Nelson on HMS *Victory* defeating thirty-three French and Spanish ships just west of Cape Trafalgar in 1805. Nelson, who was fatally wounded during the battle, was a true hero and the boys admired him tremendously.

The Admiral also spent time talking about travel to other lands, especially the New World of North and South America. He'd say the Navy was the best way to get to see the New World.

"The Navy is the safest carrier in the world. Just imagine being aboard one of those large unsinkable naval ships sailing the broad Atlantic," he would tell the boys.

Neil devoured every word the Admiral said. He was certain a life with the Navy would offer adventure and excitement. There was no doubt about it, he would become a sailor when he finished school.

The Dewar family lived on Castle Street, not far from the docks. Neil liked watching the naval ships as they came in the bay, all decked out in flags blowing in the wind, enroute to the naval port of Southampton. At school, the Admiral would often let the boys run to the windows and watch as they guessed the names of arriving ships.

In early June, Neil graduated from school at age fourteen, having completed the Royal Reader. For him to get further education he would have to go to another city. Otherwise, he would have to try to get work at the factory where his father was employed. His application for a job in the factory was on file, but he was told to go back cleaning rust covered iron until a full time position became available.

Neil wasn't happy, but he took the job because nothing else was available. In the meantime, though, he went to his teacher, the Admiral, and asked him to contact the Navy, requesting enlisting documents. The Admiral was happy to oblige.

In a couple of weeks the papers arrived. Neil filled them out with the help of the Admiral. He was concerned when he discovered he had to have his father's signature before he sent the papers to the recruiting station at Southampton.

After supper that night, Neil told his father and mother he was going to join His Majesty's Navy. Simon Dewar became very upset and threatened not to sign the papers.

"You are only fourteen, Neil," he shouted. "You are too young to leave home and go on the high seas in one of the King's ships and I'm not going to allow it. If you wait a couple more months you'll get a job in the factory... just be patient, son."

"I am going to join the Navy, Dad." Neil looked his father in the eye and spoke with determination. "I'm not going to work in the dirty rust cleaning yard any more. I'm heading out to Southampton naval school tomorrow, whether you sign the papers or not."

Simon Dewar looked at his beloved son. He knew he was a man even though he was only fourteen. Neil was tough and strong as an ox. Simon knew full well he could not keep his son around forever. The world was expanding. New lands were being discovered. With all the talk of riches being found in the Americas, he himself often thought about crossing the Atlantic.

Simon signed the papers that night.

In the early morning, Neil put his clothes bag over his shoulder, kissed his mother, and said goodbye to his father and the rest of his family. Then he marched aboard the mail steamer and headed for Southampton to join His Majesty's Navy.

Chapter 2

LEARNING HIS TRADE

Neil and five other naval recruits were met at the dock by a naval recruiting officer. The officer and his driver put the recruits into a carriage pulled by two horses and took them to the naval training academy, about ten miles distant. Southampton was a large busy city. Neil had never before seen so many people or so many ships, especially so many large freighters. He had a lot of questions he wanted to ask but he kept quiet, not wanting to be a bother.

The ride to the naval academy took several hours, with muddy roads and steep hills making for a bumpy ride. On arrival, the six recruits checked in at the administrative office, where the Duty Sergeant was less than friendly.

"Straighten up when you stand before me," he yelled at one of the recruits.

The young man almost jumped out of his boots. "Yes sir," he replied in a very mild voice.

"Now answer the questions in a clear voice. And I am not 'sir.' I am a Sergeant."

The young recruit was sixteen and it was his first time away from home, "Yes, Sergeant," he replied.

Neil was the last to check in. Although he was the youngest, he was the tallest and most physically developed.

"What's your name, young fellow," asked the Sergeant.

"Neil Dewar, Sergeant."

"How old are you?"

"I'm fourteen," Neil replied.

"Fourteen?" The Sergeant paused and looked up at him. "Fourteen, you're only fourteen? I thought you were at least twenty. Where are you from?"

"From Oakfield, but I was born in Scotland," Neil replied.

"Let's see your hands," said the Sergeant.

Neil obediently held out his hands; they were callused from hard work in the steel yard, and his fingernails were unusually worn down. The Sergeant could see that this young man was used to hard physical work. Although he was very young, he already had a man's well developed body.

"I am going to send you to a platoon that has been in training for a month," the Sergeant said after a few minutes shuffling papers around. "I think you will fit in with them fine."

Neil said nothing as the man wrote a letter and passed it to him. The carriage driver was summoned and told to take Neil to another area of the training depot and deliver him to the Sergeant in charge there. Neil picked up his clothes bag and was immediately on his way.

* * * * *

Neil was met by an Army Corporal who was in charge of teaching recruits how to properly wear a uniform and march on the parade square. Neil was accustomed to working under a boss; he had no problem with being told what to do.

The Corporal told Neil to get settled in and assigned him to a room with another trainee. Neil quickly fit in. His attitude was positive and he caught on fast. He very much wanted to become a sailor and committed himself to that end. After six weeks of basic training, Neil was selected to go aboard a civilian ship to work on an apprenticeship.

He was attached as an apprentice aboard the brig *Lord Collingwood* under Captain McLachlan and sailing out of Greenock, Scotland. The name Lord Collingwood was familar to Neil. He remembered his teacher, the Admiral, saying that Admiral Lord Collingwood was a friend of Lord Nelson and was at the Battle of Trafalgar with him. It was Collingwood who took command of the British fleet after Nelson's death. And it was Collingwood who brought the sad news of Nelson's death back to the people of England.

The brig *Lord Collingwood* was a freighter that transported cargo and supplies to ports around the west and northwest coast of the British Isles. Travelling the coast gave Neil excellent experience in navigation.

Neil was quickly learning to become a naval officer. By age sixteen, he had gained a wealth of experience and thought of himself as a seasoned sailor. He enjoyed being at sea and had no problem enduring rough conditions, including standing on deck on blustery days along the northwest coast of Scotland during the late fall.

During the two years he spent on the *Lord Collingwood*, Neil received very little pay. Just enough to exist on. It was all part of his naval training.

From the *Lord Collingwood*, he was transferred to the ocean-going *Robust* – a five-masted sailing ship under Captain Landells – to finish up the final year of his apprenticeship before going on to naval ships.

The *Robust* and three other ships were charged with the task of supplying the British Navy overseas with supplics and war material. Neil signed on as a Third Class Naval Officer. He was in charge of stores and security.

The *Robust* made several trips to South Africa and into the Mediterranean Sea. During his last tour of duty Neil was made a Second Lieutenant after the Purser became seriously ill and died. By now, he was seventeen.

When the *Robust* came back to England for a refit it, and four other ships, were assigned to a trip across the Atlantic to Kingston, Jamaica, to resupply the British forces at Port Royal naval base.

Neil was well respected aboard the *Robust*. Even though he was only seventeen he looked older and more mature, and he did any job assigned to him well. Captain Landells considered Neil his most reliable officer.

* * * * *

Landells was an experienced captain. He had been charged with the task of delivering five ships laden with much needed supplies to Jamaica, and he was determined to succeed no matter what.

The trip across the Atlantic took much longer than expected. One of the ships had a steering problem and this delayed them by nearly a week. The ships also ran into several major storms which drove them off course and separated them from each other for some considerable time. However, they all finally regrouped and made it safely into Kingston harbour.

As he approached the Caribbean Sea, Captain Landells told his crew that pirates were his greatest fear, especially when ships got separated. He said he didn't feel safe until he arrived inside Port Royal naval base.

The British war ships stationed at Port Royal patrolled the Spanish Main and had many times experienced heavy resistance from pirates. When the five supply ships arrived at Port Royal, it was learned that a British man-of-war had been sunk two days earlier, and another man-of-war had been heavily damaged with much loss of life as a result of pirates operating west of Jamaica.

Neil was curious about Port Royal. He knew that Horatio Nelson, Admiral Lord Nelson, had commanded Fort Charles in

Port Royal in 1779. He knew too that Port Royal had earlier been the headquarters for buccaneers and pirates, including the notorious Henry Morgan, who was later knighted and made Lieutenant Governor of Jamaica. Morgan died at Port Royal in 1688. A few years after his death, in 1692, an earthquake struck Port Royal and killed thousands of people. Of the six forts there, only Fort Charles was left standing.

There was a minor fuss when the five supply ships sailed into Kingston Harbour. At that time in the early eighteen hundreds there were only two quays in Kingston's inner harbour, and as a result of that a man-of-war had to move from the dock in order to make room for the arriving ships.

After the *Robust* docked and the unloading began, a group of naval officers, led by Commodore Angus, came aboard to meet with Captain Landells and deliver a message from Admiral Vane.

"We have been directed to requisition men and officers from your ships' company," said the lead officer after he had introduced his companions.

Captain Landells was aware his military personnel could be taken from him whenever the Navy requested; it was part of the bargain. But he hadn't anticipated losing men at this time and he was quick to express his concern.

"I suppose there's not much I can say about the request because these are military men and most of them have served their apprenticeships. The only problem I have is that if I lose my key men I will have difficulty managing the ships on the return trip to England."

The Captain sounded distraught but the military officers ignored him. They weren't interested in hearing his complaints. They needed men and were intent on having them.

A Lieutenant requested a list of naval men serving their apprenticeships aboard the *Robust* and Captain Landells quickly complied. On the list was the name *Second Lieutenant Neil Dewar*.

Commodore Angus immediately wanted to know why a British Navy Second Lieutenant was aboard, and why he wasn't in the regular Navy.

"Is there any reason for this naval offficer being on this civilian ship? Is he serving any kind of disciplinary action? Do you have his record aboard?" he asked.

"Yes, I have his record," replied Captain Landells. "But you can't see it."

"We demand to see it; you can't refuse us," the officer said.

"His record is in my head, sir, there is nothing on paper," said Landells.

"Then tell us about him," the officer said.

Landells knew he had to give the officers any information they requested regarding Navy men who were serving their apprenticeships with him.

"Dewar came aboard this ship two years ago," he said. "I have promoted him to Second Lieutenant and he is one of my most reliable officers. He is in charge of the stores aboard and has the responsibility of properly loading and unloading the freight on all five ships. He also keeps inventory of everything coming aboard and going ashore. He is well trained for all of these tasks."

"Does he have any skills in navigation?" asked another officer.

"Yes, as well as studying navigation and astronomy, he has spent a lot of time with me and he is very good, able to make excellent judgements," said Landells.

"Will you have him come here? We would like to speak to him. The Admiral is in need of someone with navigational skills," the officer said.

"I'll have him summoned immediately." The Captain sent word to Neil to come to his office at once. He knew the naval officers would be surprised to see such a young officer. Within minutes there was a tap on the door and Neil was told to come in. He entered without saluting, but stood to attention. The officers stared at him. He looked like an overgrown boy.

"How old are you?" an officer asked.

"Seventeen two weeks ago, sir," Neil replied.

"Who promoted you?" asked the officer in charge.

"Captain McLachlan of the brig *Lord Collingwood* and Captain Landells of this ship, sir," Neil said.

Another officer asked him where he was from.

"I am a Scotsman, my family immigrated to Oakfield on the Isle of Wight when I was very young. I was there till I was fourteen. I worked my way through school scrubbing rust off steel carriage shoes, then I went into officer's training at Southhampton. After that, I was sent to work out my apprenticeship on private ships, sir, and I ended up here."

"You look younger than seventeen," said the officer.

"I am seventeen, sir," Neil said again, adding, "Some say I look older then my age, sir."

"Why aren't you wearing a Navy uniform?" Commodore Angus asked.

Captain Landells quickly answered, "My orders, gentlemen. I told all the Navy men with me to wear civilian dress as this is a civilian ship."

There was a pause as the officers looked Neil over in a manner similar to horse buyers; they even came close to examining his teeth.

"I don't know if you have heard the news yet, Lieutenant, but we recently lost a lot of men when one of our ships went down. And another was seriously damaged in battle a few days ago. Admiral Vane now wants enough officers and ordinary sailors to man two ships. You, sir, will be transferred to one of our ships immediately," said Commodore Angus.

Neil was very surprised to hear that he would be transferred right away. He had a job to do here, to supervise the unloading of the five supply ships. However, being a naval officer he had no choice but to do whatever was ordered.

"Yes, sir, I am at your service," he replied.

"Pack your gear. You will be going ashore with us. You have half an hour," the officer in charge told him.

Neil looked at Captain Landells as if to ask his permission.

"I am no longer your boss, Lieutenant Dewar," Landells smiled as he caught Neil looking at him. "You are a servant of the King. I wish you luck in all your future endeavours. You have served this ship faithfully and I know you will do well, Lieutenant."

Neil shook hands with the Captain, saluted him and left. He never saw Captain Landells again!

Chapter 3

A CHANGE IN PLANS

Neil was very excited to be in Jamaica. It was so much different than the British Isles; the coral reefs, white sand beaches, soft balmy air, and the warm blue water of the Caribbean Sea were all beautiful beyond belief.

Neil and sixteen other men were ordered to fall in line and march ashore carrying their duffel bags. They were marched to a barracks not far from the waterfront and assigned sleeping quarters. During the late afternoon, a Captain came and told them where they were to go. Neil was assigned to HMS *Cleopatra*, under Captain Gill. He quickly learned that Gill was an experienced man who had spent his life in the Navy and taken part in many naval battles.

The *Cleopatra* was a noble ship, a frigate that had seen better times; she had been lying idle for two years in Kingston harbour. However, after the sinking of one of the Navy's best ships and the serious damage of another, the *Cleopatra* was given a refit and prepared for an assignment to Haiti. Afterwards, it was put on patrol around the Spanish Main. The *Cleopatra* was an easy ship to manage and could manoeuver in and out of ports like none other in the fleet.

* * * * *

Admiral Vane was very concerned that Neil had been promoted by civilian captains and he told Commodore Angus to demote him to an ordinary seaman.

"I wouldn't do that, sir, if I were you," said Angus.

"Why not?" Vane asked. "We don't know enough about him to allow this to continue. A Second Lieutenant has a great deal of authority and responsibility, and this boy is only seventeen."

"I would be nervous if Landells found out we demoted Dewar because of his age," said Angus. "Let's face it, he could go to the Admiralty or even the King with a letter of complaint and recommend civilian ships not have anything else to do with training naval cadets."

Admiral Vane and Commodore Angus finally came to the decision that it was best to leave Neil Dewar as he was, at least for the time being.

Not long afterwards, the *Cleopatra* and eight other war ships set off on patrol in and around the Caribbean Sea. Admiral Vane was aboard the *Cleopatra*.

First stop was Port-au-Prince, Haiti, where the Admiral met with the Haitian governor in order to settle a dispute over slaves. The convoy then set sail for Grenada. After rounding the southern end of Grenada they went east out into the Atlantic Ocean, patrolling north westward back to the western end of Cuba. The ships avoided Havana for fear of encountering the Spanish Navy, then returned to home base at Kingston.

Neil spent the next three years aboard the *Cleopatra* with Captain Gill. The *Cleopatra* acted as the flagship in a group of eight warships that patrolled the Spanish Main. The ship took the lead role whenever there was trouble, and especially when it came to chasing down the pirates who were continually harassing ships carrying gold and silver back to Europe.

After three years cruising the Spanish Main, the *Cleopatra* and her crew were ordered back to Southampton. The ship's tour of duty was declared finished, and she was retired as a fighting ship and returned to service as a training vessel.

Neil was transferred to a battleship, *HMS Sophia*, for a further six months. Aboard was Admiral Vane, who made it very clear to Neil that he was too young to have the rank of full Lieutenant. Vane ordered that a written message be delivered to Neil. The message said:

"Lieutenant, after a careful review by my staff and I, it has been decided you do not have the experience necessary to take the responsibility of directing men in the event of one of His Majesty's ships engaging in a major sea battle. For this reason, we see fit to demote you to the rank of leading seaman, effective immediately."

Neil was shocked when he read what Admiral Vane had written. He couldn't believe the Admiral meant what he was saying. It couldn't be true. Neil requested a meeting with Admiral Vane and was refused.

He was then given a job below decks as a splicer in the rope lockers. He felt as though he had committed a crime and was being punished. The other members of the crew began asking questions about why he had been demoted. The Captain said it was simply that Admiral Vane thought Neil Dewar was too young to have the rank of a full Lieutenant and had therefore demoted him.

The men and officers aboard the ship became very upset and expressed their concerns to the Captain. They threatened to cause trouble if Neil wasn't reinstated. Admiral Vane responded by ordering the ships into Port Royal where he immediately reinstated Neil to his former rank.

Neil was then transferred to HMS *Merlin* under Captain Bolivar. The *Merlin* was taking on stores and getting ready to conduct patrols along the North Atlantic coast as far north as Nova Scotia. Neil didn't like patrolling along the American coast. He was unhappy and that led to him changing his mind about a career in the Navy. He didn't tell anyone what he was thinking, but he was pleased when the *Merlin* was ordered back to Southampton.

On arrival at Southampton, Neil's tour of duty as a naval officer was over. He had signed on for five years and served six because of overseas duties. By now he was a full Lieutenant, but he continued to be very disturbed at the way he had been treated by Admiral Vane. After the *Merlin* docked, Neil went to Captain Bolivar and advised him of his intention to resign from the Navy.

"I'm sorry to see you leave, Lieutenant," said Bolivar. "You have been a good and reliable officer. I'm sure the problem you experienced with Admiral Vane will soon be forgotten and you can move on."

"Sir, I have made up my mind. I am terminating my term of duty in the British Navy immediately, or as soon as you see fit, hopefully today." Neil spoke resolutely; he had no intention of being swayed from his decision.

Captain Bolivar realized Neil was serious, and no doubt, he thought, he himself would do the same if he had received such shabby treatment.

"I will fill out your request and send it ashore to head office immediately," he told Neil, who thanked him, saluted, and left.

At approximately twelve hundred hours the next day, Neil Dewar was discharged from the *Merlin*. He walked down the gangplank to the dock as a civilian. His plan was to board the mail steamer and go home to Oakfield on the Isle of Wight.

Chapter 4
TO CANADA

The mail steamer made the trip to Oakfield in just over twelve hours. It was 10 a.m. when it docked at the long pier that stretched out into the water for more than five hundred yards. Neil noticed nothing had changed, except that the faces of the men who caught the lines looked a little older. He suddenly realized he had been away from this place for over seven years. Neil had written his mother several times, especially when he was in Jamaica. He had received three letters from her in all that time.

Neil had been a boy when he left and now he was a man. He didn't think people on the dock would recognize him. However, he recognized a few of the men working there, as well as a woman who was seeing someone off. When the catwalk was lowered, Neil came ashore carrying a kit bag in one hand and a package in the other, a gift for his mother.

In the seven years that Neil had been gone not a day passed that Maggie Dewar did not think about him. But she hadn't heard from her boy now in over a year. On this particular day, Simon had gone to work early and the two girls were at the clothing factory where they were employed. Maggie was home alone. She was in the kitchen with the window open. Neil glimpsed her and called to her from the roadway. Maggie was washing clothes in the wooden wash tub when she heard what she was sure was

Neil's voice. Startled, and thinking her imagination was playing tricks on her, she straightened up and looked around.

"Mom, it's me, Neil, I'm home," Neil called from the road again.

Maggie tried to stay calm and not panic. She was sure it was Neil's voice she was hearing. But how could that be? He was at sea!

Her heart was racing as she rushed to open the door. She couldn't believe her eyes when she saw Neil walking up the pathway. Her son was back home! Her boy was home safe and sound. She kissed and hugged him, realizing with a pang that the boy who had gone away seven years ago was now a full grown man.

They sat in the kitchen and she peppered him with questions. She wanted to know everything he had done and everywhere he had been since he had left home. They sat and talked for hours. When he told her about Jamaica she was fascinated.

Neil was informed that his father wasn't feeling well. He had been spitting blood for over six months and had lost weight. The doctor said he had a lung infection caused from working in the steel mill. Maggie said Simon wasn't sure how long more he was going to be able to continue working.

Neil felt devastated by the news about his father. His father had been a strong, healthy, vibrant man when he left home. Now his future looked grim.

* * * * *

After three days at home visiting with his family and catching up with all the news from his parents and two younger sisters, Neil felt it was time for him to get back to work. When a ship called the *Langton* came to Oakfield to pick up freight for ports along the northeast coast of England and Norway, he signed on as Purser.

The *Langton* spent most of the winter going from port to port around the North Sea and carrying freight and passengers. The weather was bad and icing up was the biggest problem, particularly along the north coast of Norway. The ship went as far north as Bergen, Norway's second largest city. Neil stayed on the *Langton* until September, but he had no intention of spending another winter around the cold North Sea.

After the ship docked at Greenock, Scotland, he decided to leave. He went to the office, did the necessary paperwork, and the company discharged him. He immediately joined another ship, the *Montreal*, as third officer in charge of stores. The ship, under Captain Rayside, was loading for Montreal, Canada.

It was fall by now and Neil knew the sea would be rough in the North Atlantic, especially around the Labrador Sea. He was told the *Montreal*, which was owned by a company in the Canadian city of Quebec, would make one trip to Canada then return to Spain and spend the rest of the winter cruising the African coast. With the promise of warm, sunny weather in his future, he knew he would be able to handle the cold he had to deal with first.

THE PLACE CALLED QUIRPON

Chapter 5
THE MONTREAL

The *Montreal* was a five-masted ship built of oak. It was four years old, and had been used as a military supply ship for the British on ocean going voyages between Europe and America. Captain Rayside was in his late fifties. He was an ex-military officer who had spent his entire career around the Indian Ocean and left most of the decision making to his first officer.

The *Montreal* was not a very well run ship. It was dirty and needed new paint, likely explaining why there were vacancies aboard. Neil joined simply because it was going south around Africa in the winter. It seemed Captain Rayside wasn't much concerned about what went on aboard the ship. He was happy-go-lucky and left everything to the First Mate.

Neil was surprised to see several women berthed in the Captain's cabin. One day, after the ship left port, he asked the Boatswain who the women were; he was sure the Captain didn't have three wives.

"They are the skipper's women," the Boatswain winked. "Captain Rayside likes to say these women are in training. They travel with him all the time. He doesn't share them with anyone, not even the Mate."

"I wonder if he'd let me in on the deal?" Neil grinned.

"I'll give you some good advice," the Boatswain was suddenly serious. "Don't even let the thought enter your head if you know what's good for you."

Neil said nothing more. He had no intention of entering the Captain's cabin or getting involved with his women.

The *Montreal* was a rowdy ship. Over half the crew were Portugese. Young and out for adventure, some couldn't speak English. The Captain wasn't concerned about the amount of liquor aboard ship or what went on below deck. His only concern was getting safely from port to port, and getting the freight on and off on time.

The *Montreal* went past the north coast of Ireland and headed on a westerly course across the Atlantic. There was a fair wind from the north and all her canvases were in the breeze. The man aloft yelled, "All is well, Mate," as the bass rope strained and every knot and block tightened from the pressure of the moving air.

Everything appeared to be smooth sailing aboard. The sailors on watch checked their ropes periodically, sometimes taking in slack or lengthening more out, depending on changing squalls or changing pitch on the steerage. Other sailors dozed below, dressed in their oilskins and ready to respond at a moment's notice. As an officer with a knowledge of navigation, Neil was required to spend most of his time on the bridge. Everyone had to answer to the Mate, who seemed to be on duty at all times.

In mid-Atlantic, the *Montreal* encountered a heavy gale from the northwest and was forced to move in a southwest direction for three days. The Mate looked worried. He had made only one trip across the Atlantic before, entering Canadian waters through the Strait of Belle Isle. Having to sail in the direction they were now heading would put them a great distance off course to the south. He told his officers he would have to sail back north when the wind came in his favour and pick up the westerly course again.

Neil said that would not be necessary.

"You can go on a westerly course around the south coast of Newfoundland now, then through the Cabot Strait and into the Gulf of St Lawrence, and on to Montreal," he told the Mate, who was relieved to accept his advice. Neil continued, "I have been on Navy ships that have done that route and it is a better one at this time of year. Further north, temperatures are colder and there's always fear of the ship icing up."

One night, not long afterwards, a bunch of sailors got into a drunken brawl. A few days before, Neil had reported to the Mate that some sailors were running off moonshine from molasses beer. The Mate reported this to the Captain who dismissed it without checking any further. During the brawl, a fight broke out between British and Portuguese sailors. Several sailors received knife wounds serious enough to put them out of action. Neil was sent below to restore order and try to find out what had happened. The situation was such that finally the Captain had to be called. He threatened to put the men responsible for the trouble ashore on an island or set them adrift in a dory if any more trouble erupted.

After that incident, the *Montreal* waited several days to get fair wind for the trip into the Gulf of St. Lawrence. The winds blew from the west and northwest almost continously. But finally it changed to the northeast. Fair wind all the way to Montreal!

THE PLACE CALLED QUIRPON

Chapter 6

THE REBECCA

The *Montreal* finally unloaded its cargo and prepared to sail back to England. Captain Rayside decided to leave the troublemaking sailors, who now said they were going to desert, in Montreal. He informed company officials he wasn't prepared to take the ship back across the Atlantic with the troublemakers aboard.

By now, Neil had had enough of the *Montreal* and its slack captain. He went to Captain Rayside and advised him that he wasn't prepared to stay aboard his ship for the return voyage.

"I would rather live with the natives here in Canada than stay on your ship. I'm leaving, thank you very much," he told him.

The company paid Neil his outstanding wages. As he walked away from the ship, he was surprised to see that four other members of the crew had joined him.

The five men walked out on the dock, jobless. But they weren't unemployed long. They soon met Captain Maxwell of the schooner *Rebecca*. Maxwell was looking for a crew.

Neil acted as spokesman for the five man group.

"We are looking for work," he told the Captain. He also explained why the men had left the *Montreal*. "We couldn't take it any longer, we were afraid of a riot or something worse."

Captain Maxwell was forty-four years old. He had been on the sea from the time he was fifteen, mostly in the Caribbean. He had tangled with pirate Henry Morgan and lived to tell the tale. Maxwell was a fearless man. Everyone who knew him liked him. He was the kind of man who gave reasonable people a reasonable deal. He saw something good in the men who had experienced such misadventure on the Montreal and he advised the company officials to hire them.

The officials interviewed the men. They were satisfied with Neil's qualifications, and were especially impressed with his book-keeping skills. He was hired to keep account of all freight coming aboard the ship. The other men were hired upon his recommendation.

The company gave orders to Captain Maxwell to sail to Cape Charles, Labrador, to pick up a partial load of salt bulk cod. The cod had been landed by American bankers in late August for a group of American privateers with premises there. The residents of Cape Charles had cleaned, salted, and partly dried the catch. After loading the fish, the *Rebecca*, a four-masted schooner, was to go to Harrington Harbour on the Quebec North Shore and load barrels of herring, then sail for Montreal.

"The herring is owned by an American firm located in Boston in the United States," said the company manager. "You will unload the barrels of herring here in Montreal, but not the cod fish. Then you will go to Cape Charles and finish loading the remainder of the salt cod and proceed across the Atlantic to Cadiz, Spain."

Captain Maxwell was puzzled. He wasn't sure if the company officials knew what they were doing.

"Why can't we go to Cape Charles, take on the full load of fish, then go on across the Atlantic?" he asked. "That's better than having to come back here with a half cargo of herring, then beat it back to Cape Charles and finish loading the salt cod. Getting into those small places at this time of the year is a major challenge."

"As you know, Captain, we only have one vessel in this area now and that's yours," said the manager. "The company wants the herring brought here from Harrington Harbour so that it can go on the market. We will give you cash to pay the fishermen in Harrington Harbour and in Cape Charles. We will also give you winter supplies for the people in both places. You can give cash for what they don't take in supplies."

Maxwell had no choice but to accept company orders.

"When we get to Spain how will we know where to go from there?" he asked.

"The company has an office in Cadiz and I think they will be sending you to North Africa for a cargo of some sort, perhaps one bound for New York."

"I hope this has nothing to do with the slave trade. I got into enough trouble the last time I was in that kind of business," grumbled Maxwell.

"The *Rebecca* is owned by an American company based in London, England; the Americans will tell you what to do," said the manager.

Maxwell didn't like what he was hearing.

"If the men find out we have to go somewhere in Africa for a load of slaves they might jump ship," he said. "There are still a lot of hard feelings because of the American Revolutionary War and that slave racket."

"Don't worry about it – maybe it's a load of salt you will have to bring back," said the manager.

Captain Maxwell asked no more questions as he started preparing for the voyage to Cape Charles, Labrador.

* * * * *

Cape Charles is a small inlet protected by three large islands and several smaller ones on the south coast of Labrador. The island closest to the shore is Charles Island, the middle one is Seal Island, with Caribou Run separating them, the third island is Bottle Island. The only way for a vessel the size of the Rebecca to get into Cape Charles harbour is through Caribou Run. Cape Charles was first occupied by Dorset Eskimoes who migrated further north after white settlers arrived. Nicholas Darby, a Bristol merchant, took over Cape Charles in 1765. In 1770, it was occupied by George Cartwright, another English adventurer. During the 1770s, English fishermen from Newfoundland came to Cape Charles, fishing inshore for cod, herring, and salmon and selling their catches to American buyers.

* * * * *

Neil had never been to the Labrador coast, although he had heard many stories about the land God gave to Cain, as some called it. When he'd been on a Navy ship heading for North America, with its course set through the Strait of Belle Isle, the big talk was of massive icebergs and the Labrador current that swallowed everything that touched its surface. He had heard from experienced men about the horror of the Labrador Sea, the roughest and the most unforgiving place in the world. Ships dreaded to go there, but the lucrative fishing grounds surrounding the Labrador coast were the best in North America. They were, in fact, the best in the world, and for that reason men were attracted to the coast in every kind of boat imaginable. Neil Dewar was now heading to Labrador and he was excited!

Captain Maxwell took on enough stores and supplies for the trip to Cape Charles. He expected to make the voyage in two weeks, depending on the weather, of course. His greatest worry was not having enough men to load the fish when they got to Cape Charles. He wasn't sure there would be any inhabitants there this late in October. Labrador people usually moved further into the bay for the winter months and went trapping animals for meat and fur. Captain Maxwell expressed his concerns to the company manager who obliged by sending extra men with hand-barrows to help load the fish.

In the early morning of October 8,1816, the *Rebecca* set sail for Cape Charles with a fair wind. It was smooth sailing down the St. Lawrence River and out into the Gulf. However, things soon changed with a heavy northeast gale, and the *Rebecca* made for Port Menier on Anticosti Island and anchored for two days to wait out the storm.

The wind finally came around from the southwest. This was fair wind for the schooner as it set sail around the east side of Anticosti Island and then northeast along the west coast of Newfoundland. Although the *Rebecca* encountered heavy seas and foggy weather, it finally slipped like a floating cork in a bottle into Cape Charles Harbour, three days after leaving Anticosti Island.

Captain Maxwell gave a great sigh of relief as he dropped anchor near the rickety wharf and threw the lines. Jack Brown, the company foreman in Cape Charles, was there to greet the schooner, as were all the inhabitants of the small fishing settlement. Maxwell was happy to see they hadn't yet left for their winter homes in the bay.

"Captain, you should turn the schooner around before you start loading," Jack shouted from the wharf. "There's not much water beneath her where you are now."

Jack was familiar with the Labrador coast and the Northern Peninsula of Newfoundland; he had travelled to both areas frequently as a fish buyer. Maxwell thought for a moment then realized what Jack had said.

"He's right," he told the Mate. "We'll turn her around. When it's time to go we will just have to hoist the canvas, untie her, and head straight out the harbour, provided the wind is in our favour."

Jack signalled to the Captain from the wharf.

"I want to see you," he yelled through cupped hands. "Can you come ashore for a minute?"

"Sure thing, I'll be right down," Maxwell said. Then he turned to Neil, "Dewar, I have to go and pay off the inshore men. But, in the meantime, you can get started with your job. Get half the men ashore with hand-barrows and wheelbarrows. Get whatever fish you can out to where we can reach it with the block and tackle and start hoisting it aboard."

Maxwell paid the people who worked curing the fish on shore before any of it was moved. Afterwards, Neil started loading the *Rebecca*. By now it was severely cold. Although the fish was heavily salted and had two days drying, most of it was frozen and hard to bend.

With Neil overseeing operations, it took only a day and a half for the men, women, and youngsters to half-load the *Rebecca* and have her ready to get underway. The weather cooperated, it was cold but sunny.

As dawn broke, the wind was northwest, blowing straight out the harbour and Captain Maxwell was ready to go. He was well informed about the shoals he had to manoeuver to exit the harbour. Jack Brown had told him the way to go.

After slipping the lines and saying farewell, in less than fifteen minutes the *Rebecca* was out of sight, running with full sail through the run and heading for Harrington Harbour.

The ship was at Harrington Harbour for two days before the loading of herring was completed. The barrels of herring weighed three hundred pounds and stowing them below deck was pure slavery. Even hoisting them aboard the schooner was back-breaking labour.

The wind continued to blow hard from the northwest, with snow flurries causing ice everywhere on the schooner. The ice made the vessel top heavy and Captain Maxwell was afraid it would capsize. He had to make a run for Anticosti Island where he put in at Port Menier and beat off the ice; this took a full day. It was late in the evening when the wind came around from the northeast.

"We have to set sail right away, this is fair wind up the Gulf," Captain Maxwell told the Mate. "By noon tomorrow, we should be close to Montreal if the wind stays northeast the way it is now."

"I agree," said the Mate. "I think it's warming up too, so we might not get as much icing."

It was a little after 4 p.m. when the *Rebecca* sailed into Montreal harbour. Captain Maxwell and the crew were happy to get into port.

Chapter 7
CAPE CHARLES, LABRADOR

In Montreal, Captain Maxwell was called to the company office and given the outline of his next voyage.

"You are to go back to Cape Charles and pick up the remainder of the salt fish, then head across the Atlantic to Cadiz, Spain," the manager informed him.

"I hope the families in Cape Charles haven't moved in to Lewis Bay for the winter yet. Jack Brown told us everyone would be moving as soon as the fish was shipped. Jack was having a problem keeping them back even before we arrived," said Maxwell.

"Its important for you to get back there as soon as possible," said the manager.

"If the people have left it will take our crew a long time to get the freight loaded," answered Maxwell.

"There will be six men as well as four women and four children going with you as passengers. The men have agreed to help you load the fish," said the manager.

Captain Maxwell was surprised. He wasn't expecting to be carrying women and youngsters on a trip at this time of year. He asked where the women and children would sleep and the manager said he knew the Captain would find a place for them. He said all the two of them had to do was follow orders and do what they were told.

Captain Maxwell wasn't pleased, but he didn't say anything else. The manager was right, they had to follow orders. But getting quarters for the women and children would be a problem. The Captain told Neil to get enough stores aboard to last the crew and passengers for two months. He said they would fill their water tanks when they got to Cape Charles. Captain Maxwell stressed they had to get on the move; there was no time to lose.

"What do you think of the weather?" Neil asked.

"We are in for southwest wind, that's fair wind. I don't know how long it will last but we have to capitalize on it. The wind could push us a long way out of the Gulf," Maxwell answered.

"Skipper, I don't like the look of that Cape Charles harbour and with the wind northwest or northeast, we could have a big problem trying to beat our way in," said the Mate.

"Yes, I figured that out last week when we were there. Northwest wind blows out of the harbour, and it's the same with the wind northeast. 'Tis poison," said the Captain.

With the wind southwest, the temperature went up and that encouraged Captain Maxwell to set sail immediately.

The *Rebecca* cast off her lines and spread her sails as she headed out towards the Gulf of St. Lawrence, on her way again towards Cape Charles, Labrador. It was November 8, 1816.

Chapter 8
CHATEAU BAY

The *Rebecca* experienced rough seas in the Gulf of St. Lawrence. She was tossed to and fro but handled herself quite well. The half-load she carried stabilized her; she didn't roll as much as when empty. Late in the evening of the second day, Captain Maxwell noticed the wind coming around from the northwest.

"I think we are going to have a norwester, the sky looks wild," he said to the Mate. "I think we'll head into port."

The Mate unrolled the chart he had been studying since leaving Montreal. He had made notes and marked each place they passed.

"We are off Mutton Bay, Quebec North Shore, about four miles," he told Maxwell. "The anchorage looks good, according to the chart."

"We should be able to beat our way in before dark even if the wind does pick up to a stiff breeze," Maxwell said.

"I guess we don't have much choice," Neil spoke up. He'd been studying the chart with the Mate. "We can't keep going in this all night especially if it turns cold."

"Once we get around Big Dike Island, according to the chart, everything should be all right," said the Mate.

Captain Maxwell nodded. "Pull her in toward Mutton Bay. We shouldn't have too many problems getting in there."

"Captain, I think we should run about another mile ahead," Neil suggested. "It will give us more room on the leeward shore in case we get a sudden squall from the northwest."

Maxwell agreed. It took less than two hours for the *Rebecca* to beat its way into Mutton Bay, where the water was as calm as a bathtub. The ship anchored for two days waiting out the northwest gale.

Captain Maxwell decided to get out of Mutton Bay early on the third day.

"We can't keep waiting for the wind to come around," he said to the Mate. "It's better for us to beat around on the open ocean than here in this pond. Out there, we can go in any direction. In here, we can't move."

The *Rebecca* got out of Mutton Bay around Mecatina Island, and then put out into the Gulf of St. Lawrence. It was November 13.

"It's the thirteenth of the month so it's good it's not Friday," Captain Maxwell said with a laugh. No one commented.

"When I was on the Navy ship *Robust* I often heard old Captain Landells say that a southeaster was always in debt to a northwester, and he was always right," said Neil.

"What did he mean by that?" asked the Mate.

"It means if the wind blows from the northwest it's guaranteed to blow back from exactly the opposite point on the compass and that's southeast. We've marked it time and and time again," said Neil.

"If that's the case, we should be in for a real gale of southeast wind. We've had the wind northwest now for a week or so," said the Mate.

"Getting in somewhere out of a gale of southeast wind is not an easy task over here on the west side of the Strait of Belle Isle," said Maxwell.

"There's only one other place I know of and that's Red Bay. If we can get in there we'll be safe enough." The Mate nodded with certainty.

"Okay, let's head that way. At the first sign the wind is on the land from the southeast or southern, we'll head for Red Bay," said Maxwell.

During the afternoon, the sky started to cloud over and the wind came around from the south.

"There's no doubt about it, we are going to have the wind in from the southeast, there's a shift in the sails," said the Mate, as he looked up in the rigging.

Captain Maxwell came on deck to take a look and he could tell a storm was brewing.

"Swing her in for Red Bay and we should have pretty good going. The wind is in our favour to go into the wharf," he said. "It will be good to get the women and youngsters ashore for a while, let them have a walk around and stretch their legs."

This was on November 14.

By the time the *Rebecca* had her lines ashore it had started to rain and it was obvious a storm was brewing.

When the people of Red Bay found out there were women and children on board the schooner they came to the wharf and took them to their homes and kept them overnight. It gave the passengers a break from living aboard the rolling vessel; one of the women said it saved her life.

After two days waiting out the storm at Red Bay, the *Rebecca* got under sail in a stiff westerly breeze. There were a few problems getting out from the inner harbour with a side wind. However, there was nothing the crew couldn't handle, even though a heavy sea was rolling in from the southeast after the storm. Undertow kicked up from the high waves was pounding the cliffs and the ocean seemed as though it was boiling. The westerly wind was picking up strength and Captain Maxwell knew this would push back the heavy seas. By noon, the west wind was dropping, so was the sea.

Around 2 p.m. it came to the attention of the Captain that the children aboard were seasick because the ship was rolling so much in the heavy seas. A decision was made to go into Chateau Bay for a few hours to give the passengers a break. Neil was not happy with this decision. He told Captain Maxwell they were only about twenty miles from Cape Charles. He said it was important to push full steam ahead and make it to Cape Charles before there was a change in the wind. The Captain and Mate ignored him.

It seemed to Neil that Captain Maxwell was having an affair with one of the women passengers. He'd also noticed that the Mate was more than friendly with another woman. There wasn't anything he could do about it, just be silent.

After the *Rebecca* entered Chateau Bay the wind dropped to a dead calm. In fact, with all the canvas up it barely pushed her into position for anchorage at Henley Harbour. Neil urged Captain Maxwell to turn the vessel around with her head pointing out the harbour, and put a heavy line ashore from the stern. He suggested as well that two extra anchors be dropped, one on each side in the event the wind come northwest. It was fortunate the Captain agreed because at midnight the wind came northwest, at hurricane strength.

"Captain, you and the Mate can turn in and I'll take the shift tonight with ten of the sailors. If we have trouble I'll give you a call," Neil said and they both gladly agreed.

During the night it started to snow, and with the heavy wind it created a blizzard. The Mate was awakened at dawn and told of the conditions outside.

"It's bitter cold with blowing snow. I think we should wait a few hours before moving, the wind may slack off after the sun gets higher. In the meantime, we have to get the snow shovelled from the deck and shake salt around to make it safe getting around," said Neil.

"Let me check things out with the Captain and see what he has to say," said the Mate.

Neil waited and finally the Mate came back to say the Captain would soon come on deck and make a decision. After Captain Maxwell came on deck and had a look he called Neil below to view the charts and asked him what was the distance to Cape Charles.

"About twenty miles according to the chart, that is after we get out from here and around Banks Island," said Neil.

"What do you think we should do?" Maxwell asked.

"I think we should stay here another twenty-four hours, or at least wait till the wind dies down. You can't get in through Caribou Run with the wind northwest, we proved that when we were there the other day, sir," said Neil.

"I think we should move on, Captain. If we can't get in when we get there we may be able to run ahead to Battle Harbour and wait there," said the Mate.

Neil was in no position to start an argument with the Mate. He shouldn't have even been discussing the running of the vessel with the Captain. "Maybe the Mate knows best, but I doubt it," he thought to himself.

"Okay, start taking in the anchors and get the canvas on her, I'm going to have breakfast," said Maxwell.

In less than an hour, the crew had the *Rebecca* ready to sail from Chateau Bay into the stormy Strait of Belle Isle.

THE PLACE CALLED QUIRPON

Chapter 9
MEETING EMILY

Except for the spray freezing on the ship, the trip going northeast along the Southern Labrador coast wasn't too bad. However, Neil and the Captain knew there was no way they would be able to get into Cape Charles with the wind in this direction. It would be next to suicide.

It was now November 17.

As the *Rebecca* approached Gull Island off Cape Charles, Neil advised the Captain to keep inside the island.

"We will be closer to Caribou Run after we get past the island," he said. "And, you never know, but there could be a delay in the wind as we get there. We might be able to dart her on inside safely."

"No, keep her outside," said the Mate. "It's too risky to go inside Gull Island. If the wind increases when we're halfway through the run, Skipper, you know what could happen then."

"Yes. I agree with you, Mate. The wind is almost hurricane force now, so keep her off," said Maxwell.

Neil couldn't understand the decisions the Captain and Mate were making and he wasn't sure they were the right ones. It was obvious from the approach via Caribou Run that it would be next too impossible to get inside without crashing on the rocks. The winds were too strong and blowing out the harbour. There was no room for the *Rebecca* to carry sail to beat the vessel in through. It was only in the nick of time that they avoided crashing on the rocks outside. Neil was amazed at the Captain and the Mate's confusion when it came to making decisions. From now on, he thought, they would have to be watched closely or the vessel could get in serious trouble.

After being unsuccessful at making Cape Charles harbour, the *Rebecca* proceeded further to the northeast and let down its anchor. This area was between Bottle Island and Seal Island. From here, the ship could be seen by people on the islands.

"Hoist the Union Jack upside down, let them know we're in distress," said the worried Captain.

Jack Brown and a group of men saw the distress signal and knew it was the *Rebecca*. They were expecting her.

"Something is wrong out there, men," said Jack. "The wind is in the wrong direction to come in the harbour and there's nothing we can do about it. They should pull up anchor and go up to Lewis Bay."

Jack got the signal flag and he and a group of men walked up over the hill in order to get nearer to the schooner. They signalled back, saying they could offer no assistance, only to suggest the schooner go to a sheltered area. Captain Maxwell understood the signals.

Neil couldn't understand what the signals were all about. The *Rebecca* was not in distress, or in any immediate danger, it was only delayed in getting into the harbour. Maxwell signalled back that he was going to stay where he was until the wind changed.

"Captain, you can't stay here," protested Neil. "If the holding ground isn't good you could drift a hundred miles off shore before daylight. Why can't you run further ahead and up into St. Lewis Bay? No wind can hurt you on the back of one of them islands. It's like a pond there, it's the place for you to wait out the storm. Look at the chart again."

Captain Maxwell took another look at the chart and decided to take Neil's advice and go into St Lewis Bay. By the time the *Rebecca* got in around one of the islands it was beginning to get dark.

"Captain," said Neil. "We should put a line around one of them big boulders ashore just to be on the safe side. And put an extra anchor out up to the northeast."

"I don't know about a line ashore, but an extra anchor might be all right," Maxwell responded. "Get a few men in the jolly boat and run one out." (A jolly boat is a small boat approximately 16 feet long with two sets of oars that is used for going ashore when the ship is anchored.)

Around 8 p.m. the wind started dropping. By now, the moon was out and Neil noticed a heavy ring around it.

"That means bad weather or a hurricane of wind," he said to himself as he looked up at the evening sky. Out loud he said, "We should make a move now, Captain. It's a light night and by the time we get out around Seal Island there should be no problem getting into Cape Charles harbour."

The Mate spoke up: "We should wait till daylight, night has no eyes, the wind shouldn't breeze till after the sun comes up."

"Have you seen the glass? It's bottom up," said Neil.

"It has been bottom up all week if you ask me." Captain Maxwell sounded glum.

"I think we are going to get a heavy northeaster." Neil was determined to speak his mind.

"No," said the Mate. "You won't be getting the wind northeast after all the northwest wind we've had. No, sir, to go fooling around this time of night is not wise. If we strike a shoal what will we have then, the bottom tore out of her?"

Captain Maxwell was silent, but he seemed to be in agreement with the Mate. Neil didn't like it, but there wasn't anything he could do except wait. Fed up, he decided to go lie down in his bunk. Around midnight or a little after, he got up and went out on deck.

He knew what was happening as soon as he opened the companion door. Drifting snow hit him in the face! The *Rebecca* was headed into the wind and it was northeast. He called to the men on watch and asked what time the storm had come on.

"About an hour ago, sir," one of the men answered. "We gave the anchor slack and let her tail with the wind. The three anchors appear to be holding quite well. We're checking with the sounders every few minutes to make sure we're not dragging."

"Go get a couple more men," said Neil. "We have to make sure we don't drag. If we do, we'll drop the heavy anchor."

Neil went below and informed the Mate about conditions on deck. "You can't see fifty feet for drifting snow and I'm worried about the vessel dragging her anchors," he said. "We should have put the heavy line ashore like I suggested. That way we couldn't drift."

"Can you handle things on deck, Purser?" the Mate sounded bored.

"Yes. If I find her dragging her anchors I'll give you a call." Neil felt like giving the Mate a poke.

"Okay," said the Mate, and he pulled the rug up over his head.

The night was long and the storm continued to get worse. Neil told the men to exercise safety precautions while using the lead sinkers along the railing.

"Make sure you work in pairs," he cautioned. "If we lose a man overboard in those conditions, it will be impossible to launch a boat to retrieve him."

There was no sea heaving because the schooner was too far in among the islands, but the wind whistling in the rigging was like a thousand violins playing.

As the dawn broke, the men on night shift went below and had breakfast and retired to their bunks. The men replacing them on day shift were told to clean the snow from the deck and to make sure it stayed cleared. By now, land was visible and it wasn't necessary to use the lead sinkers.

Captain Maxwell came on deck and looked around. "What do you think of the situation now, Dewar?" he asked.

"This wind isn't going to let up all day, and we are in for a heavy snowfall," said Neil. "As long as the anchors hold and no one falls overboard we are all right. That is, if we don't do anything crazy."

"You can go below and eat now, Dewar. The women have a nice breakfast made for you," Maxwell said as he pulled the hood on his coat around his ears.

The Mate came up from below with a sour look on his face. Neil figured something had gone wrong, but he knew it had nothing to do with the running of the schooner because the Mate had not been on deck. Down below, Neil went into the lavatory when one of the women came out. A lantern hanging from the ceiling was turned up high giving lots of light. He shut the door and noticed everything was very clean, "A woman's touch," he muttered, as he got a jug of water from the hose in the corner and washed. Although he felt tired after a gruelling night, the wash refreshed him. Feeling better, he went to the table and was served a great breakfast of porridge and salt fish.

Three of the women were busy with the children and one woman tended on Neil, making sure he was enjoying his meal. The woman looking after him was beautiful, with long brown hair and big blue eyes. Neil found it hard not to stare at her. He heard one of the other women call her Emily, and he thought the name was as pretty as she was.

The women wanted to know all about him, where he was from, where he had been, how old he was, if he was married, and anything else that came to their mind. Neil told them everything they wanted to know. After talking to them for half an hour, he thanked them for the satisfying breakfast, saved a special smile for Emily, and went down to his bunk.

The storm continued all day. At times, Captain Maxwell estimated the wind was sixty to seventy knots an hour.

"We're lucky we are in among those islands," he said to Neil that evening. "On the outside of this bay the sea must be mountainious."

"I have no doubt you are right," said Neil, then added, "This storm could continue with no let-up for a week."

"Why do you say that?" asked Maxwell.

"When we were in Cape Charles I had a long talk with Jack Brown about the weather. He's spent his life here and he said he had seen storms last for weeks at this time of the year. They call them the November gales. That's the reason they all go into Lewis Bay in October before the bad weather comes on. He said they would have all been gone inland by now if not for the fish they had to ship. They could't go because they had to have their money for food," said Neil.

"I've never seen the like before," said Maxwell. "It has been blowing every day, even before we left Montreal. Jack must be right."

"It's the time of the year, and the fact that we've got to get into one of them rock holes here on this coast, that's what makes it so bad," said Neil. "If we were out on the open ocean we would be having a very good time of it, even in this breeze."

Captain Maxwell put his elbows on the table and sighed, then whispered, "I suppose it's true for whoever said it: this must be the land God gave to Cain."

Neil laughed!

"It's like it everywhere this time of the year, Skipper, all along the eastern seaboard. This is the stormy season. We're in a safe place now and our anchors are holding firm. Let's wait out the storm, wait for a good time."

"I suppose you're right, it's almost like God's pocket in here," said Maxwell.

"At the first sign of the weather clearing or the wind off the land, we should up anchors and head for Cape Charles. We might get in the harbour," said the Mate.

"It's not the wind off the land we need to get in through Caribou Run," Neil said. "It's the wind in on the land, from southwest to southeast. Anything else is contrary and you'd be taking a big chance."

"Whatever it takes, we'll wait for the proper wind direction. It's better to do that than end up on the rocks," said Maxwell.

For three days and nights, the *Rebecca* lay at anchor in a steady northeast gale with heavy snow. The storm was so severe that heavy seas were even beginning to be felt in St. Lewis Bay. The schooner was covered in a sheet of ice all the way from the waterline to the railing. The crew were kept busy shovelling snow and beating off the ice that was covering everything. Neil had never seen the like before, especially the piercing winds. On the morning of the third day, it started to lighten up and the northeast wind began to drop.

"Looks like it's going to clear," Neil told the Captain.

"I think it's about time. Tell the men to get ready to hoist in the anchors, we're getting out of here this morning supposing we have to go back to Montreal," Captain Maxwell sounded frustrated.

The Mate told the Captain to wait until the sea outside the bay dropped.

"I'd say with the heavy sea that's kicked up by this northeast storm Caribou Run is breaking with every cast of the sea," he said. "If that's the case, you won't be able to get through. So we should wait at least two or three hours until the sea goes back."

Neil was frustrated. "And if we wait till the sea goes back and the wind picks up from the northwest, we still won't get in through Caribou Run. I think we should go on now," he said.

"Dewar, have the men take in two of the anchors. Let her swing on one and we'll see what happens," said Maxwell.

Neil went on deck and gave orders to lift two anchors. The men hoisted the two main anchors aboard and Neil noticed the vessel starting to swing around.

"The wind is coming around from the northwest, fair wind out the bay," said a sailor who was standing near him.

"You're right," Neil answered. "We have to start getting the canvas up."

"Should I tell the men to start now?" The sailor sounded anxious.

"Not yet. I have to clear it with the Captain first." Neil went below to report to the Captain. "Will we start hoisting the sails, sir?" he asked.

"No, not yet," Maxwell answered. "Not until we see what's going to happen. It might be just a baffle back from the hills."

In less than an hour the wind from the northwest started picking up. The Mate came on deck, looked around, and ordered the remaining anchor pulled in and the sails hoisted. He said they were going to see if they could get into Cape Charles.

Knowing he had no choice but to obey, Neil relayed the orders to the men and turned the *Rebecca* out of the bay, even though he knew there was too much wind to get into Cape Charles harbour.

In about an hour the schooner was out in the Strait of Belle Isle. The heavy swell was crashing against the cliffs, churning up a foamy undertow that floated out at least two hundred yards. It was easy to see that the storm had released its fury with a vengeance.

As the *Rebecca* came out of the bay, Neil could see small houses huddled on the barren hillside. The land and everything on it was frozen and there wasn't a tree for miles. But the people in the houses were alive; he could see smoke coming up through the stove pipes. The Captain ordered the ship's horn to be blown several times to let the people know it was still in the area. Through the drifting snow, the men standing at the rail could see people come out of their houses and wave their hands in greeting.

As the schooner got close to the entrance to Caribou Run it was obvious it was futile to try to enter the harbour. Instead, Captain Maxwell decided to go near Gull Island and heave to. He ordered one of the anchors let down, and said they would stay and see what happened. They would wait until at least 3 p.m.

Everyone aboard was nervous. The wind was almost hurricane force, at least sixty knots. Neil noticed fast moving clouds with strings of snow dangling from them reaching to the low hills like a reaper's long rake. The sun was setting, darkness was rolling in.

As the *Rebecca* rolled in the heavy sea, Neil leaned on the rail and gazed at the wild sky, wondering what the next twenty-four hours would bring.

"We can't keep this vessel here all night, it's too dangerous," he said out loud, "I wonder what the Skipper's got in mind?"

Hearing someone behind him he quickly turned and was surprised to see one of the women passengers standing on deck.

"You'd better be careful, ma'am. You could get blown overboard up here. This ship is being tossed around like an eggshell," he said.

"I'm sick and tired of being below, shut up in that stinking hole with a bunch of lunatics, not knowing whether I'm going to live or die. I hate it. Can't someone tell me what's going on?" The woman's knuckles were white as she tightly gripped the railing.

Neil glanced at her. He couldn't see her face. She was wearing a heavy coat with the hood pulled up and had kid gloves on her hands.

"I'm only the Purser, ma'am. I don't make the decisions. It's the Captain and the Mate who handle things," he told her.

"I came to Montreal to visit my aunt and my father purchased my ticket back to England. But no one told us anything about coming to Labrador to get a load of fish on the way across the Atlantic." Her voice rose in anger. "For God's sake, can't someone beat some sense into the Captain's brain, if he's got one, that is, and get him to forget about trying to get into that damn place for a few fish."

Neil knew the woman was perfectly right; it was time to move on. However, he wasn't in any position to comment. He told her to talk it over with the Captain.

"Talk it over with the Captain," she repeated.

Neil knew from the way she spoke that she had more to say.

Just then, a gust of wind blew the woman's hood down and he saw it was Emily. The girl who had served him breakfast was even more beautiful than when he'd first seen her.

"Are you aware of what's going on down below at night while you are up here on watch?" Her face flushed in anger as she spoke. "The Captain and the Mate each have a woman in their bunks. I see it all. If my father had suspected something like that was going to happen on this ship he would not have let me come aboard."

"I don't think I should comment on any of that. It might cause quite a disturbance if the crew found out about it. It's better for you to say nothing either, at least until we get across the Atlantic," he told her.

"My name is Emily Cummings," she said with a sudden smile that made dimples appear in both her cheeks. "And you told us over breakfast that you are Neil Dewar. So, Neil, I think

I'll stay here on deck with you for a while, it might not be nice but at least I'll get fresh air."

"You can't stay here, Emily, one wrong move and you could go over the side."

"Do you know what you should do now, Neil?" She was looking at him very intently. "You should take control of this ship and do the right thing. It may save our lives."

"I can't take control of this ship, Emily. If I did, I would be charged with mutiny if I ever got into port."

"You may regret not doing it. If you do decide to do it, I will defend you in any court." She moved closer to him and put one hand on his arm. "Neil, I have to ask a favour of you. If anything happens to this ship will you save my life? My father will reward you, he has businesses in London and Montreal. He is very well to do."

He didn't answer, he couldn't answer.

She waited a few minutes to get a reply; when none came she asked him if it was true that he wasn't married. He said he wasn't and never had been.

"I don't know what I'll do when I get to Spain," she said. "I just know I will be leaving this contraption of a boat as soon as I can get my feet on the ground. Where will you be going when we get to Spain?"

"I'm not quite sure where I'll go, but I'll be doing the same as you. I'll be leaving this vessel the minute it arrives in port. I've had enough too."

"You and I should team up and head for London together," she said with an impish grin.

"I'm not sure where I'll go, it all depends if I get paid right away. And if I do, I am going to England for sure. Yes, maybe I could join you in London."

Neil looked into her blue eyes and thought how wonderful it would be to be in London with her. They could go to plays, walk in the park, sit in restaurants and sip wine, rent a horse and buggy and go on a picnic in the country. Maybe, just maybe, if all went well they would end up together forever. They would marry and have children, two or three or four. They would have a wonderful life, he and Emily and the children. Neil's gaze was faraway as he contemplated the dream.

"Don't worry about money," Emily smiled and her dimples appeared again. "I have enough for you and I to go around Europe twice."

Neil thought for a minute, then replied, "When we get to Cape Charles we will go ashore. I have a friend there, Jack Brown. We will visit his home and make plans."

"Neil Dewar, you have a date," she said happily.

She put one arm in his and leaned close to kiss him on the cheek. The kiss was soft and gentle and sweet. Neil turned and looked deep into her eyes as he put his arms around her and held her tight. Their lips met and they stood, locked in an embrace neither wanted ever to end, as the boat rocked beneath their feet and the wild wind blew all around them.

"You had better go below, Emily," Neil said after a long while. "It would not look good for someone to see me kissing you here on deck."

"I'm not going to worry about that. But I will go below if you promise faithfully to come and let me make you a cup of tea when you are finished your shift."

"That would be lovely," he said, giving her yet another kiss.

Neil looked up at the evening sky. He could tell it was going to be a very wild night; he felt the storm was getting worse. Emily edged closer and gripped his arm.

"Down below, Neil... the Captain and the Mate... it's not just them and the women. They are drinking down there too. It frightens me."

"It's just as I suspected," Neil whispered softly. "Maybe the Captain and the Mate don't want to get into Cape Charles because they are having too good a time out here."

Emily put her head on his shoulder and he leaned over to kiss her yet again.

"I'm frightened, Neil, I don't know what to do," she said.

"Don't be frightened, it won't help you. Just keep your nerve up and say nothing. I will help in any way I can."

She was trembling and tears were running down her face as he held her tight and gently pushed her windblown hair out of her face. He kept an arm around her as he walked her to the companionway where they kissed and said goodnight.

"Just until I see you again," she whispered.

* * * * *

Minutes after Emily had gone below, Captain Maxwell came on deck and looked at the evening sky.

"The sky is wild," he said. "I have to say I don't like the look of things. What do you think, Neil?"

"To tell the truth, I don't know what to think. The sun sank in a bank of heavy clouds and that usually calls for wind from the northeast or southeast. And if it's the case we're in a bad spot, not one bit of protection in the world." Neil paused for a second, then added, "You wouldn't have enough anchors this side of the Azores to hold her from drifting in a gale like we've had in the last three days."

"It's too late to go back to St Lewis Bay. It's better to let her drift if the wind comes northeast."

"Let her drift, Captain?" Neil was incredulous. "You can't do that, sir, it's too dangerous. It's against every navigational rule in the book."

Neil spoke sternly and Captain Maxwell didn't like it. No one talked to him like that, especially a Purser.

"Listen, Neil Dewar," he said in an angry tight voice. "I make the decisions aboard this ship. From now on you'll only comment when I ask you something."

"I'm sorry, Skipper. I didn't mean to be condescending. Sorry. I apologize."

"I know it's frustrating. You spend all your time on deck, it's tough." Maxwell relented.

"It's my duty," Neil replied, and then he eagerly continued on with what he wanted to say. "We don't have to go back to Lewis Bay, sir! I was looking at the chart and we can go into a small harbour on Camp Bay Island, five miles from here to the southwest. We could be there before darkness sets in if we left now."

Maxwell thought for a moment then replied, "I'll run this by the Mate, see what he thinks of it."

The Captain went below and didn't come back till dark. When he arrived back on deck he surveyed the situation as he walked along the rail. Neil was having a discussion with two of the men near the forward hatch. Maxwell called out to him.

"You called me, sir?" Neil came over.

"Yes," Maxwell replied. "I ran what you said by the Mate and he thinks it's better to hold on here. If the wind comes around from the northeast we'll let her drift if the anchors don't hold."

Neil knew there was no use arguing, or trying to persuade the Captain otherwise.

"Okay, sir, if that's your order," he said.

It was his last real conversation with Captain Maxwell.

Chapter 10
DISASTER

At 9 p.m. the sky was overcast and it was pitch black.

The men on deck knew another storm was brewing from the way the heavy cloud bank appeared in the eastern sky. They were also aware of the orders the Captain had given Neil about letting the vessel drift. It was not a wise decision as far as they were concerned, especially here in the Strait of Belle Isle! Things would be different if the vessel was in mid-Atlantic. The current that swept through this waterway at the changing of the tides resulted in many vessels going to their doom along the rocky coastline, even in broad daylight.

Earlier in the evening, before darkness closed in, Neil had closely studied the lie of the land, both along the Labrador Coast and along the Newfoundland side. If the vessel had to drift, it would have to go in a direction out towards the center of the Straits. If not, there was a chance it could be swept among the many shoals that guarded Chateau Bay on one side, and the many shoals near Flowers Cove on the Newfoundland side.

However, with the tide boiling northward, Neil knew if the wind came on strong from the northeast or southeast there would be a turmoil in the center of the Straits.

"If we had gone in around Camp Bay Islands when I wanted to this afternoon we would be safe there," Neil told the man standing at the wheel. "But now we don't know about the

situation. In fact, I'm puzzled as to where I would set a course....
We'll just have to wait and see."

Just before midnight, the wind came on from the northeast
with heavy snow. Captain Maxwell was called on deck to have a
look.

"What direction did you say the wind was?" he asked Neil.

"It's northeast, sir," he replied.

"Are you sure? It appears to be southeast to me."

"No, it's northeast, sir. I checked the compass a few minutes
ago."

"How many anchors have you got out?"

"Two. If you put out any more you may damage the deck."

Maxwell knew Neil was right! He had seen it happen before.

"Okay, leave it at that," he said. "If she starts to drag pull in
the anchors and we'll drift."

Captain Maxwell was dressed in a long heavy coat with a cap
tied under his chin and a scarf around his neck. The leather gloves
he wore came halfway up to his elbows.

There was no doubt the man could be tough when needed.
But, thought Neil, on this voyage, well, perhaps it was the woman
he was having an affair with who had got the better of him.

As Maxwell looked around he knew the *Rebecca* could be in
trouble. The blinding snow and the darkness combined with the
roar of wind in the rigging gave him an uneasy feeling.

He knew there wasn't much use having the anchors out near
Cape Charles Gull Island; it was just as well to lift them from the
bottom and let her drift. Shortly afterwards, he gave orders to lift
the anchors.

"We should drop an anchor from the starboard side about two
thirds back first, sir," Neil suggested. "That way, we will be able
to turn the vessel around and have her drift heading down wind.
If we don't, the rudder won't be much good to her."

"Yes, get her around," Maxwell yelled above the wind.

After the *Rebecca* got on the move, the sea started to mount. As Neil had surmised, the wind and the tide running against it made the sea very rough.

By now, the Mate was on deck, wearing warm, heavy clothes and looking nervous. He asked Neil several questions which got lost in the roar of the wind. After a considerable time, he made it clear he wanted to know if Neil had any idea how fast the vessel was travelling.

"I don't know," said Neil. "There's a heavy tide running in the opposite direction and that's slowing us down."

"Do you have any idea how far we are off shore?" The Mate stepped closer to Neil to ask his question.

"No, not the faintest idea," Neil answered. "All I know is that we are somewhere in the Strait of Belle Isle, drifting ahead to somewhere. We can't see ten feet with the snow."

The Mate said nothing as Neil continued, "If I was in charge I would hoist the mainsail and head northwest. At least then we wouldn't go on the rocks on the Newfoundland side."

"We are not going to do that," the Mate sounded annoyed. "Just let her drift like she's going." A minute later the Mate had gone below.

Just after 3 a.m. the wind changed again, back to the northwest. The snow continued to come in swirls, covering everything. Neil checked the compass.

"Sure enough, we are heading in a southeasterly direction, almost a side roll from the waves coming from the northeast," he told the man at the wheel. "I am going to call the Mate, someone has to make a decision."

He called below and in a few minutes the Mate came up on deck. "Listen," Neil said as soon as he saw him. "You have to pay attention to me for a minute. The wind is tripping from the northwest or northerly."

"It's northwest, according to the direction of the sea," said the Mate.

"We have got to be careful about this," said Neil. "If we have driven further to the southwest than we think there's a danger of striking land somewhere along the west side of the Northern Peninsula. Because of that, I think we should hoist a couple of sails and beat further east or go on up to the southwest. It's better to be in any of them areas than ashore on the rocks."

"I don't think we've gone as far west as that," said the Mate. "I'll see what the Skipper has to say."

Captain Maxwell was just coming on deck.

"I'll be with you in a minute," he responded to the Mate as he started looking up into the rigging and talking to a couple of men about the watch up front. He needed men up there watching and listening for anything that might appear out of the darkness.

As soon as the Captain finished talking, the Mate spoke up. "Dewar suggests we hoist a couple of sails and take a course to the southwest and keep out in the center of the Strait."

"Does he have any idea where we are?"

"No, and that's the reason he thinks we should run more to the southwest."

"I'm puzzled as to what to do," said Captain Maxwell. "But I don't think we went all that far to the southwest while we were drifting under bare poles. I don't think we went far enough to put us in any danger of colliding with the shoreline going in this direction."

"Maybe you're right. But I'm worried, it's like navigating with your eyes closed." The Mate sounded anxious.

"We are in this mess now, Mate, and we have got to try and get through it." Captain Maxwell paused. "Make sure everyone is on alert and have a man go up in the front rigging. He may see better there than down below... and double the starboard watch."

Neil had a feeling that something awful was going to happen. A foreboding, his mother would have said. There was no need of them being in this situation, he thought. The *Rebecca* could be anchored in one of the bays along the Labrador coast right now if only the Captain had listened to common sense earlier in the day.

Earlier in the evening, while they were anchored near Gull Island, Neil had sized up the life boats. They were the dory type, about twenty feet long and probably built when the vessel was under construction. Stacked aboard each life boat was a sixteen foot jolly boat, used for going ashore while the ship was anchored. Neil noticed the larger life boats were in need of repairs.

One of these sets of boats was within reach of the area where the officer on watch spent most of his time. Neil looked at the boats and then at a sailor and said, "If an emergency came and we had to use one of them dories, I wouldn't want to be one of the people aboard."

"That's how it is aboard those vessels, no one cares," the sailor replied.

Neil saw that the jolly boats weren't even strapped down. They had been hoisted aboard and left as was. It was a wonder they hadn't been tossed over the side with all the rolling of the schooner.

* * * * *

The Captain looked at his pocket watch. He was anxious for daylight to break.

"It's only 4 a.m." he said to Neil and the Mate. "Four more hours before daylight. I don't like running under bare poles. You don't have much control of the vessel, better to have at least one sail in the wind. Look here, the snow is turning to heavy squalls of hail and sleet. You can't see ten feet."

"Listen," Neil held up one hand. "I think I hear something."
"So do I."
The Mate cocked his head to one side and listened.
"It sounded like a clap of thunder," he said.
In a split second they heard a chilling cry from the watch up in the rigging.
"All hands on deck, men, we are going on the rocks!"
It was a cry no mariner ever wants to hear.
It is a cry that puts fear in the heart of each and every sailor.

Chapter 11

SIX REMAINING MEN

It was only a matter of seconds before the *Rebecca* met her doom.

It seemed as though a giant hand picked her up and slammed her headfirst into the solid granite cliffs on a point of land less than half a mile east off Cape Norman.

Even before the men in the forecastle heard the warning cry, the head of the schooner struck with such tremendous violence that the two forward masts broke off close to the deck and fell over the side.

Captain Maxwell heard the awful screams of the man in the mast as he fell to his death in the boiling crashing sea. The Captain started yelling, but no one heard him. The *Rebecca* was like a wounded bucking steer in a stampede.

Neil heard women and children screaming from down below. He roared at the Mate to get them up on deck as he rushed to help Captain Maxwell launch the jolly boats.

A passenger by the name of Roy Thompson and three of the crew had just come up from the forecastle and their eyes bulged in disbelief at what was happening. They heard the Captain yelling and ran to help launch the jolly boat.

It was a dreadful situation, waves were pushing the vessel closer to the jagged cliffs. Every time a wave rolled in and hit her, the sound of broken timbers could be heard like gunshots.

The situation was desperate. It seemed as though it was the end for all souls aboard.

Captain Maxwell and Neil, together with Roy Thompson and the others, quickly launched a jolly boat, but before anyone could get aboard it filled with water from another breaking wave and was swept away. The Captain and his helpers rushed toward the lifeboat.

The *Rebecca* was again hit hard by a violent wave that smashed it into the cliff and crushed it all the way back to the forecastle. The crushed front of the vessel lay close to the cliff when the sea ran back. Thompson and the three crew members with him left the Captain and ran to the front of the schooner in the hope of getting ashore from the bowsprit. However, a giant wave came and washed them away.

When the sea ran back from the cliff, the rear of the schoooner went under and water filled the Captain's quarters. Neil heard the screams of women and children again.

It was then he heard Emily's voice: "Neil, Neil help me. I am going to be lost if you don't help me, I'm over here."

Neil turned and saw her. She was holding on to a rope dangling from the rigging and debris was everywhere, tossed around by the raging sea. He made a dash for her, but a huge wave swept the deck and she was washed overboard. His heart broke as he saw her bobbing in the swirling undertow and then she was swept from his reach and disappeared into the darkness all around.

That was the last anyone saw of the women and children. They all perished in a watery grave.

* * * * *

Standing there, peering into the blackness into which Emily had disappeared, Neil knew his duty was to try and save as many of the others as he could.

As water poured out of the smashed forecastle, he saw several bodies float out with it. Desperation was setting in. He turned his attention to the lifeboat the Captain and his helpers had readied and jumped aboard just as a massive wave struck the *Rebecca*, turning it side on to the cliff.

For a moment, it seemed it would roll over but instead it was held in an upright position for a few seconds until the sea ran back. This time, the stern of the vessel stayed up in the cliff, causing what was left of the bow section to go underwater. Neil saw that the rear section of the keel and part of the bottom were tangled in the jagged rocks below, completely torn off and separated from the vessel.

He saw two men holding onto the rigging; they were standing on the port side with their legs wrapped around the rope ladder going up into the spar. It was Charley Donaldson and Richard McFie. There was no use calling to them. Nothing could be heard above the roar of the sea and the wind. Neil waved at them to come aboard the lifeboat and they immediately jumped from the spar into the boat.

"Who's got a knife? Quick, for God's sake, cut the straps." Neil roared as he saw that the straps holding the lifeboat to the deck were still intact. Donaldson produced a knife and Neil grabbed it as he jumped like a cat and cut the straps just as another wave hit the *Rebecca*.

Just then he heard someone scream and turned to see Captain Maxwell pulling a man into the lifeboat. Donaldson pulled in someone else. The two men pulled in were the Mate and a young sailor. The wave that hit the *Rebecca* at that moment swept the lifeboat from the deck and slammed it into the cliff, crushing one of its sides.

"Hold on tight, men," Neil yelled loudly as another wave rolled in. The wave picked up the lifeboat as if it were a toy and threw it again towards the cliff.

However, instead of smashing into the cliff, the lifeboat went all the way over the ledge to the other side of the point. It landed upright in the water about twenty feet below.

Captain Maxwell lay flat in the bottom of the lifeboat; he appeared to be injured.

In the place where they landed on the other side of the reef, Neil noticed a lot of debris and he did a quick check for other survivors. There were none.

"Grab the oars, men, and scull her off from the rocks, we may stand a chance," he yelled.

Donaldson and McFie each quickly caught an oar and started pulling the lifeboat off from the land. As they pulled the boat further from the breaking sea, Neil saw they were in the shelter of the point. While the waves were still large, they were not as big as they had been and this made it easier to get further out.

As they moved further off from the shore they could hear a woman screaming for help.

"Neil, Neil, where are you, can you save me?"

Neil immediately recognized Emily's voice and knew she must be holding onto something and trying to stay afloat. He screamed her name, once, twice and then a third time. He wanted her to call again so that he could try to find her. But as hard as he listened, not another sound was heard.

"Can we get back to the wreck? I have to get back to the wreck." Neil was frantic. "That was Emily calling. I have to get back and try to save her. I have to get back."

"We will do no such thing," the Mate spoke up. "We're damn lucky to save ourselves."

Tears came to Neil's eyes as he and the others listened, but they heard nothing more except for the roar of wind and sea. Neil knew Emily was gone. His dreams had vanished in the sea.

As they swirled in the undertow dangerously close to the foaming cliffs, they heard a man calling further off shore.

"We can't help him, we may die ourselves," said the Mate.

"Try and scull further off shore, we may see him," said Neil.

"Keep this lifeboat in a straight line as much as possible. Be careful or it might capsize. Whoever is out there has to make it on their own," said Maxwell.

"What are you saying, Captain?" Neil couldn't believe what he was hearing.

"Whoever is out there needs help and we might be able to save them so keep the boat further off."

Neil stood up and called twice. But over the roar of the waves breaking nothing could be heard. It was the last they heard from whoever it was.

*****

The seven men in the partly crushed lifeboat were experiencing high waves, blowing snow, and freezing temperatures. The Mate asked Neil where he thought they were.

"I don't know for sure," he replied, "and we won't know till daylight, if we even know then."

"We are on the Newfoundland side of the Strait of Belle Isle," the Mate sounded certain.

"There's no doubt about that, Mate. Remember what I told you about an hour ago. If you had listened, we would not have gone on the rocks, but you shrugged it off as foolishness," said Neil.

The Mate knew Neil was right; he should have listened.

Neil paid no more attention to the Mate, concentrating instead on getting Captain Maxwell up out of the water in the bottom of the boat.

"I think I've got a broken leg, and my arm hurts terribly too," Maxwell groaned.

"You'll be all right, Skipper," Neil tried to be encouraging, but he knew Maxwell was not in good shape.

As the noise from the breaking sea faded in the distance, it began to sink in that they had so far survived the wreck of the *Rebecca*. But what lay ahead they dreaded to think about.

* * * * *

Bright stars overhead were almost obscured by drifting snow as daylight broke.

Someone said, "I can hear the sea roaring up ahead." It was then that everyone strained their eyes hoping to catch a glimpse of what lay in front of them.

"Must be land somewhere up ahead not far away. There's heave-back from the land," said Neil.

Suddenly the breaking sea was in sight, and before they could blink an eye they were caught in the undertow.

"We're going to go crashing on the rocks, everyone for themselves," Neil roared.

The lifeboat was swept into a gulch by a high wave. At the end of the gulch was a pumbley-rocky beach, different from where the *Rebecca* went ashore. The lifeboat turned over as soon as it came in contact with the rocks, dumping the seven men in the freezing surf. The beach was covered in ice, causing a terrible problem as they tried to stand up.

Neil was the first to reach the shore. The sea threw him against rocks that were covered in jagged ice and he was stunned as he struck his head. As he shook his head from side to side he recovered his senses and was conscious of a terrible pain in his knees and elbows.

His companions were crying for help all around him, but there was nothing he could do. For the moment, he was unable to stand. He noticed Captain Maxwell in the water nearby holding on to a boulder. He wasn't saying anything, but he looked terrified. In the semi-darkness, he saw McFie pulling men ashore.

Neil was out of the water, but he was aware that at any minute a wave could roll in and suck him out of the cove. He had to move! He rose on his hands and started dragging himself across the ice and snow to a higher place away from the raging sea. He found himself on a flat surface in the soft snow. He had made it safely ashore. Captain Maxwell was not far from him and he started calling to Neil to help him.

"I think I've got my two knees broken, Skipper," said Neil. "But hold on, I will try to get to you in a minute."

"I can't hold onto the rocks, they're too slippery. If you give me your hand I may make it," Maxwell begged.

Neil had to try and crawl regardless of the pain in his knees. This was his Captain who needed him. At the moment, the past and any disagreements they'd had were forgotten. He pushed himself up on his knees. The pain made him dizzy but he had to move. He crawled to the Captain, who was nearly out of the water and covered in slob ice. Neil reached out his hand and grabbed the sleeve of his coat and pulled him ashore. The two men lay there, gasping for breath. The roar of the sea was deafening.

Neil tried to stand. He got up on one knee and felt for broken bones. Finding none, he stood up. He felt the other knee and discovered the skin torn to the bone but not broken. He felt his elbows, they were torn to the bone but not broken, although he did feel the sticky flow of blood. He reached down and helped Maxwell to his feet.

"Where are the other men?" Maxwell asked.

"I heard McFie calling to someone over there."

The two men stumbled arm in arm towards what looked like shapes of men some distance away.

"Did everyone get ashore," Maxwell asked.

"There are five of us here," answered McFie.

"There are seven of us then. Thank God we made it ashore," said Maxwell.

"One of the men is in bad shape, swallowed a lot of salt water, he can hardly stand up," said McFie.

"Try to do the best you can to save him. We are going to have to huddle together," said Maxwell.

"This gulch is providing us a little shelter. If we can keep from freezing, we may be able to survive here until it gets full light," said Neil.

"We are going to have to keep jumping around to keep our blood moving," said the Mate, and the others nodded in agreement.

The seven of them were soaking wet. It wouldn't take their clothes long to freeze, especially if they went from the gulch and up into the wind. They were all aware of that.

The men had no idea where they were, but they thanked God they had made it ashore in one piece.

"It will be light very soon now and we may see something. We may even find a place where we can find shelter and dry our clothes," Neil tried to be hopeful.

"There could be woods around that will provide shelter from the high wind," said McFie.

The optimism expressed raised everyone's spirits.

"In about half an hour it will be daylight," said Maxwell.

They all knew they had to do whatever it took to stay alive in such a terrible situation. Their wet clothes stuck to their bodies and were beginning to freeze.

Neil was wearing ankle high leather boots. He could feel the water squishing around inside and knew he would have to take them off to empty them. He urged the men to stand around him for shelter while he took them off.

Although his socks were still wet, it felt better with his boots emptied out. Every one of the other men did the same thing in turn, all except for the sailor who was in such bad shape. Neil did it for him.

All the men were wearing heavy caps with flaps coming down around their face and tied with a string under their chins. Captain Maxwell and the Mate had hoods on their coats.

After half an hour huddled together in a circle with their arms around each other as they tried to shelter the injured sailor they realized he was dying. His clothes were frozen in a solid mass and he couldn't speak. When they asked him questions there was no response. Donaldson knelt close to him and heard a faint heartbeat. A few minutes later he stopped breathing.

"The man is dead," Donaldson said. "May God have mercy on his soul."

The six remaining men wondered who would be next.

* * * * *

At daybreak, the men were still alive but in bad shape.

The sea continued to roar not far away from them. The drifting snow from the rocks a few feet above their heads made the situation even worse, if such a thing was possible.

In the light of day, they noticed that the tide had gone out and left much debris floating in the cove.

Chapter 12

CHERRY BRANDY AND HARD TACK

Some of the pain was gone from Neil's knees, but his elbows were still painful. The worst of all was the numbness in his feet, they were frozen with the cold.

As it got light, some of the men were screaming with pain from frozen hands. The Mate was in the worst shape; his coat was stiff with frost and his gloves were frozen onto his hands. Captain Maxwell seemed the most fortunate of the remaining six. As the morning wore on the men could see around the cove where they had landed. Captain Maxwell pointed to some debris not far from where they were huddled together.

"That looks like one of our casks of cherry brandy over there," he said.

"I hope to God it is," said Donaldson.

Neil moved across the beach and over the slippery, icy rocks to where the cask was. He rubbed the snow off the head of the cask with his coat sleeve and looked at the writing on it.

"It's a cask of cherry brandy all right, twenty gallons of the stuff," he said, and the others cheered.

Neil looked more closely at the debris and thought he saw a bag of something being tossed in the waves. He recognized it as a sack of hard bread. (Hard bread or ship-biscuit is thick, oval shaped biscuit, baked without salt and kiln-dried, and packed in fifty pound burlap bags for ships on ocean going voyages.) Neil called to Donaldson and Maxwell to come and retrieve the sack of hard bread. He said his hands were too numb to hold onto anything, and this was their only chance to get something to eat.

The two men moved along the beach towards him, it was very slippery and hard going.

"There it is!" Donaldson shouted as he saw what Neil was pointing at. "When it gets closer after the next sea we can grab the end."

He watched the sea and when the sack came in he stepped out into the water and got hold of it. Between him and Maxwell, they managed to drag the sack out of the water. It was soaking wet.

"At least we've got something to chew on to keep us alive for a few days," said Maxwell.

Neil caught sight of one of the oars in the water near the beach. Donaldson went into the water to his knees and retrieved it. There were a lot of other things they could have used but they were too far out to get hold of.

Maxwell and Donaldson rolled the cask of cherry brandy further in on the beach to keep it safe. Then they took off their boots, emptied them out, and wrung out their socks. It was still stormy, with blowing snow, but the daylight made everything seem better.

"I think we should have some of the brandy," said the Mate. The Captain agreed.

"I am going to have a look around and see where we are," said Neil.

"I'll go with you," said Donaldson.

The two men walked up on the plateau from the cove. They were surprised to find they were on an island about a quarter of a mile away from what looked like another much larger island. The island they landed on was Green Island, the larger one was Brandy Island.

The island they were on was no larger than a quarter of a mile in diameter. They walked across it and saw no way to get to the larger island, except by boat. Once they were on the larger island they might be able to get to the mainland. In order to escape they needed a boat.

"I guess we've had it, Neil. There's no way we can get off this island unless the ocean freezes over and by then we'll all be frozen," Donaldson was despondent.

"It doesn't look very good for us, we're nearly frozen now." Neil took another look around.

Through the drifting snow he could see another headland further to the southeast, about three or four miles away. This headland was Raleigh Cape, but that way was out of the question for them.

"If only we could have saved the dory," said Neil. "Even though it was badly damaged we might have been able to repair it enough to get us across the quarter of a mile to the next island."

"The dory may have come ashore on the back of this island. I think we should have a look around," said Donaldson.

"I was thinking the same. We must keep our hopes up," Neil was optimistic but then the reality of their situation sank in and he added, "I'm sure I've got my two feet frozen solid, they are numb up to my ankles. My fingers were frozen last night but they're thawed now and blisters are starting to form on them."

"My feet are the same way," said Donaldson. "If only we had a little fire, just enough to dry our feet and hands."

"We had better go back and tell the Captain where we are. He will want to know what we found," said Neil.

"I don't have the heart to tell him," said Donaldson. "You better go by yourself."

When Neil arrived back to where the rest of the men were he could tell something was amiss. Captain Maxwell waved him over.

"Three bodies washed ashore not far from where we found the cask of cherry brandy," he said. "One of them is the fellow who tried to get ashore when the vessel struck the cliff head-first."

He and Neil walked to the beach to look at the bodies. Neil recognized the two sailors and the male passenger. He said they would have to bury them somehow.

"We won't be able to dig a grave, we don't have the tools," said Maxwell.

"All we can do is pack rocks on them so that at least the wild animals won't be able to carry them away," said Neil.

"I think the Mate can read the burial," said Maxwell.

As they walked back to the other three men huddled together near the low cliff, Neil told the Captain the bad news about what they had discovered. They were on an island with no hopes of escape.

"The Mate is in bad shape. Don't tell him until later, he might not be able to take it," said Maxwell.

"I am going to have another look around, Captain. Maybe you should come with me."

Maxwell said he would, and as they were talking they heard Donaldson calling. Thinking he was in trouble, they moved to a better vantage point. Donaldson was waving to them from about a hundred feet away and pointing to something in another cove. They hurried to him as best they could.

"Look! Look! It's the jolly boat! She's in on the beach in the next cove and looks in very good shape," Donaldson was excited.

Neil and Maxwell could hardly believe what he was saying. They thought Donaldson was seeing things. The three of them rushed to the beach and, sure enough, the jolly boat lay on its side at the high tide mark. It was half submerged in water but hardly damaged.

With half-frozen hands, the men knocked the plug out of the back of the boat and slowly drained the water. There were no oars left in the boat, just a bailer and a gaff hook which were tied on.

"We can use this boat for a shelter from the wind until the storm is over, then we can head out," said Donaldson.

Maxwell agreed. He knew it would be foolhardy to venture out in this high wind. They used the gaff hook to beat up the ice that clung to the sides of the jolly boat.

"We have to get the boat in the correct position to protect us from the wind. We can turn it partly over and put rocks and snow around it and that might provide us with shelter," said Neil.

"Let's go and get the others," said Maxwell.

The three of them hurried as best they could to tell the others. The news encouraged everyone.

* * * * *

Arm in arm, the six men walked slowly to the jolly boat. They helped each other, especially the Mate and the sailor who was in the worst shape. Richard McFie now appeared to be in the best shape of the six of them.

It was hard work to get the jolly boat turned up. They stacked rocks along the edge to keep one side of the boat up. It was quite a job to get rocks near the beach as they were frozen together.

After the boat was lifted about three feet and secured, they pulled the weakest man under it, then had to help the Mate get inside. The other four started looking for more rocks, or any kind of material to put around the boat to prevent the wind from blowing underneath, but found very little. They knew they had to find something to stop the wind blowing on them in order to save the life of the sailor and the Mate. Without shelter, they wouldn't last long. It was four hundred feet from the cove where they had come ashore to where they had found the jolly boat.

"There's enough rocks there if we could get them brought over, but it's a big task," said Neil.

"Let's take a look," said Donaldson.

The four men walked over to where they had spent the night.

"We'll have to roll the cask of cherry brandy to the boat, and drag the sack of hard bread and the oar across too," said Neil.

"We can do that later," Maxwell said. "Right now our greatest problem is getting something around the jolly boat to stop the wind. I don't think the Mate will last much longer if we can't get him some shelter."

"There's nothing we can do as far as getting rocks carried across to the boat. All the rocks are frozen together where the water came in over them. They are one solid mass," said Donaldson.

"I know what we are going to have to do," said Neil. "We've got four bodies. Why can't we drag them across to the boat and use them instead of rocks?"

"Good grief, man, do you know what you're saying?" Maxwell looked shocked.

Neil didn't know what to say. Maybe he shouldn't have suggested such a thing.

Donaldson offered to pull the bodies over.

"If you touch one of them bodies, I'll report you to the authorities the minute I get back to England," Maxwell sounded fierce.

"So, Captain Maxwell, you intend to get back to England, do you, sir?" asked Donaldson.

"Yes, I certainly do," Maxwell replied.

"But you are not concerned if the Mate and the other sailor make it back or not. They can die if they want to as far as you are concerned." Donaldson seemed to be angry. "These four men are dead and we've got to bury them somehow. We have to bring them to where the jolly boat is anyway, so why not put them around the boat to stop the wind while we wait for the storm to be over to bury them? I'm sure they wouldn't mind."

Maxwell didn't answer. Neil and Donaldson went ahead and pulled the four bodies across and put them around the boat where they did indeed stop the wind. Then, with much difficulty, Captain Maxwell rolled the keg of cherry brandy across to the boat, and Neil and Donaldson pulled the sack of hard bread over.

By now Neil's hands were in a terrible mess, especially the backs. Blood was running from his hands and the water bladders that had formed earlier were broken. His skin was broken and several of his fingernails were hanging off. He tried to get his gloves back on but they were frozen so hard he had to discard them. He worried about his feet the most, he knew they were frozen. However, he knew he was not as bad as some of the other men, especially the Mate and the sailor who were both crying in pain.

"We all need to get something in our stomachs," said McFie. "We haven't eaten since yesterday."

"Well, we have a cask of cherry brandy, a whole twenty gallons of it," said Maxwell.

"Getting it open is the big thing. Does anyone have any suggestions?" Donaldson asked.

"We have the gaff hook. We could put the hook under the hoop and strike it with a rock, it may pop the hoop off," said Neil.

"Yes, it can be done that way, but be careful not to break the hook, it may come in handy later," said Donaldson.

Neil and McFie managed to open the keg of cherry brandy without too much difficulty using the gaff hook. McFie used his knife to open the sack of frozen hard bread.

"I would say the hard bread will taste salty because it was soaked in salt water," said Neil.

"Salty or not, I want some. I am starved," said McFie.

Neil got the bailing bucket and filled it with small amounts of cherry brandy that he passed around. McFie passed around pieces of frozen hard bread. The Mate and the sick sailor were the only ones who couldn't eat it.

There was no wind under the boat, but it was cold. Captain Maxwell said if only they had a little fire things would not be so bad. They all agreed, but there wasn't any way they could get a fire going. In late afternoon the wind picked up to hurricane force with blowing snow. There was no doubt if they had not been in the shelter of the boat they would have perished. Just before darkness came upon them, Neil and McFie brought the keg of cherry brandy inside and served out small portions in the bailing bucket.

"You can't see a hand before your face out there, there's so much snow falling," said Neil. "I wonder when this will end?"

"Could be on for a week," said Maxwell.

"It's been on for a week now, there should be a change soon," said Donaldson.

"Whenever it changes we've got to get to a more sheltered place than this," said Neil.

"Looking to the westward in across the island, it doesn't look like there's much shelter that way, that is, unless we walk for miles," said Maxwell.

"It all depends on the wind." said Neil. "We've only got one oar, we may be able to scull her down wind if the sea is not too rough."

"By tomorrow, we should have a good idea what will happen. There should be a break in the weather," Donaldson was a born optimist.

"Captain, do you remember what that fellow Jack Brown told us the evening you gave him the rum?" asked Neil.

"He told us a lot of things and most of it was lies, especially after he got half-drunk," said Maxwell.

"He said there were people living over here somewhere, they were caretakers of the French fishing rooms, in a place called Quirpon. He said they stayed there all winter. I wonder if it's true," said Neil.

"I wouldn't know, but let's hope it is as that is our only hope," said Maxwell.

During the night, the wind did not abate and the men knew if they had not found the jolly boat they would have frozen to death. Well before daylight, the Mate started shaking. During the evening the other men had tried to get him to eat some of the hard bread, but without success. Donaldson even soaked some of the hard bread in cherry brandy to take away the salt taste. But all his efforts were to no avail. The Mate couldn't eat the hard bread, he urged when it came close to his mouth.

Captain Maxwell gently asked the Mate if there was anything he wanted to say, any message he wanted passed on to his family. Very faintly, the Mate whispered, "Tell Rose Marie I love her." Maxwell promised he would. Those were the Mate's last words before he went into convulsions and died. He perished from cold and hunger. No one knew who Rose Marie was.

They put the Mate outside the jolly boat and wrapped his body around the corner of the boat to help break the wind sweeping the land.

Now, five survivors were left.

* * * * *

As the sun came up on the second day, the men observed a heavy sea rolling. Everyone had sore, frozen hands and feet. While his damaged elbows and knees were no longer bleeding, Neil did have blood oozing from the backs of both of his hands. He cut off part of his shirt and bandaged his hands after releasing the water from the blisters that covered them. There was no use complaining, nothing could be done about it. Captain Maxwell appeared to be in worse shape than Neil. He couldn't stand without help and his feet were driving him insane.

"You have to hold on until the wind drops and we can get out of here. We may find a fishing village somewhere," Neil tried to rally him.

"I doubt if we'll find a fishing village around here," said Maxwell.

"Maybe we'll find one of the big French fishing rooms Jack Brown said are around this part of the coast," said Neil.

"I remember Jack talking about Cape Bauld," said Maxwell. "He said on a good day he could see the Cape very plainly from Cape Charles."

"If the weather improves we may see it from here because we are much closer to it now," said Neil.

It was apparent in the late afternoon that the sailor who had not eaten or hardly spoken was dying; he was in an unconscious state. Captain Maxwell tried without success to talk to him, but he did not respond and his breathing was very slow. The Captain felt his legs and found they were frozen; he knew the sailor would never see another sunrise. Before twelve that night he passed away. His body too was used as a windbreak.

* * * * *

The four souls left were confident they were going to make it. The odds might not have been good but they were all strong healthy men.

Captain Maxwell was forty-five years old and had always been in good physical condition. His fingers were now blistered and swollen, but he still had the use of his hands, and even though his feet were frozen he managed to get around with a little help.

Neil knew his feet were frozen, probably up to his ankles, but he could still walk with difficulty. He was able to use his hands, the palms were not blistered.

Donaldson knew he had his feet frozen and the backs of his

hands were blistered. However, he was a tough man, used to the cold.

Richard McFie was in the best shape of all. His hands weren't frozen, and even though he was suffering from frostbite in his feet and knees he could still get around fairly well.

During the evening, they searched in vain for rocks they could use to block the draft of the wind blowing underneath the boat.

"Men," Neil said, as it dawned on him what they should do. "We can take the clothes off the bodies and use them to cut down the draft."

'Why didn't we think of that before?" Donaldson asked.

"A brilliant idea," said McFie. "It may just keep us from freezing to death."

Captain Maxwell didn't approve, but he went along with the idea anyway. Donaldson and Neil cut the heavy coats off the bodies and brought them inside where they figured out a way to keep them up around the boat. They would make pegs from the head of the brandy keg and then, using a rock, they would hammer them tightly into a seam inside the risings of the boat and around the gunwales.

"We can ballast them down on the ground outside with rocks and snow to prevent them from blowing up and the whole thing then should be as strong as any wall," said Neil.

When they had everything done, the jolly boat was like a cabin and the wind was kept outside. Everyone felt renewed courage. Before it was completely dark, Neil suggested they take the bail bucket and scrape all the snow and ice from the ground underneath them and place it around the sides of the boat. When that was done, the marooned men sat close together and ate hard bread and drank mouthfuls of cherry brandy, hoping they would sleep.

During the night, the wind dropped. Neil awoke and all he could hear was the sound of the other men's heavy breathing. They were sleeping as soundly as if they were in their own beds at home. As he lay there, unable to sleep, he thought about the Mate and his actions aboard the *Rebecca*. Neil also wondered why Captain Maxwell had ignored his suggestion to go into Chateau Bay for the night and wait out the storm. He knew the Mate had a lot to do with the operations of the schooner, but if only the Captain had agreed with what Neil wanted him to do he was sure everyone would still be alive. But, no, Captain Maxwell listened to the advice of the Mate, which was completely wrong, and remained in a very threatening place. To drift at night with bare poles in such a dangerous place was suicidal! Maybe, thought Neil, he should have disobeyed the Captain and moved the schooner himself. But if he had done that he could have been charged with mutiny and sentenced to death when he got back to England. Now, the Mate was dead, stacked up outside the boat like a stick of firewood. Neil wondered where all this was going to end.

As he lay sleepless in the darkness, he could picture Emily's face as she practically begged him to do something about what was going on down in the Captain's quarters. But he hadn't done anything. If only he had done something, if only he had taken charge of the schooner as she had suggested, she might be still alive. Emily was beautiful and he felt he could have loved her deeply. But Emily was dead now, lying on the cold ocean floor. The thought haunted him. In a sad haze of restlessness, Neil finally drifted off to sleep.

Chapter 13

NOW ONLY THREE LEFT

Early the next morning, a little before dawn, Neil went outside. The wind was blowing from the northeast and that was not good. It was an even worse wind than a northwester; it blew straight in the cove.

Captain Maxwell was sitting up and complaining about his feet and hands and wondering what was going to happen to all of them. "Will we ever make it out of here alive?" he mused aloud.

Donaldson, who was unable to walk, crawled outside. When he returned, he reported it was snowing. He asked the Captain if he thought they should move from where they were this morning.

"I can't say," said Maxwell. "The wind sounds as though it has changed direction and is picking up."

"The wind has gone around to the northeast, blowing right in the cove," said Neil. "It's impossible to get the boat out. It's even worse than when the wind was northwest."

"I guess we'll have to spend another day here." McFie spoke quietly.

"We can't move with this wind, unless we launched the boat across the island, and that would call for the strength of a horse," said Neil.

"I can't stand up, let alone help to drag a boat across this island. And just look at my hands, they are swollen out of shape." The Captain held out his hands and the others could see they were in terrible shape, with infection setting in on the backs.

Neil knew what could happen if wounds like that weren't treated. However, there was nothing to treat them with.

The wind kept up all day and faded out as it began to get dark. They all agreed they should be able to make a move early the following morning. McFie asked what way they should go.

"It all depends on the wind," Neil answered. "If there's none, we will go to the westward which seems to be closest to the mainland. If the wind is blowing from the northwest or west we will head south to the headland and see what lies behind it."

With the wind blowing from the northeast, the temperature warmed up a little. Captain Maxwell wanted to take his boots off and have a look at his frozen feet. McFie said if he took off his boots he might not get them on again. Neil said it was too dark to see his feet, and he might damage them further if he removed his boots.

"I'll try taking one boot off and see what happens," said Maxwell. "My feet are hurting so much I think I will go out of my mind before daylight if I don't take them off. I'm going to take one boot off now. Give me a hand to pull it off, Neil."

The Captain moved to sit facing him, but when Neil tried to pull off the boot he knew the Captain was in trouble. His leg was swollen tight in his boot.

"Do you really want me to pull your boot off, Captain?" he asked. "Once it's off, you might not be able to get it back on."

"Yes, I want it off, so just pull it off," he ordered.

Neil had to tug at the boot several times to remove it. Each time he tugged, the Captain screamed and swore. Finally, the boot came off. The sock underneath was wet and felt like a sponge; water had reached halfway up the leg and frozen. The Captain couldn't see in the dark, but as he reached down his hand and touched his leg he howled in pain. McFie said he'd be better off putting his boot back on, but the Captain said his foot didn't hurt as much with the boot off. He said maybe he should remove the other one as well. Neil said if he did he would be in big trouble.

Maxwell said nothing more as he gently rubbed his leg. During the early morning, Neil had to slit the side of Maxwell's boot to get it back on as the Captain's leg and foot were swollen out of shape. Neil made a string by cutting a half-inch strip from the tail of his coat and wrapped it around the boot.

Just before dawn the men were outside observing the ocean. There was a fair breeze blowing from the northwest.

"What do you think of the conditions?" Maxwell asked Neil.

"It's not bad, we can make it if we hurry. Let's get the boat in the water. Sorry to say I can't do much. My knees and elbows are giving me a lot of pain. I can hardly stand."

The Captain was having trouble standing too. He was very shaky. "In what direction shall we go?" he asked.

"We'll go down wind," said Neil. "After we get around the high cliff it should be easier going and there will be shelter behind it. We may be close to the place called Quirpon."

The men removed the bodies from the sides of the jolly boat. They laid them out on the tall grass sticking above the snow not far from the edge of the ocean.

Captain Maxwell said they should bury the dead men before they left, but the others said that was impossible.

The men removed the rocks holding up the jolly boat and let it fall flat on the snow covered ground. They turned the boat over and Neil replaced the plug in the back. McFie put the keg of cherry brandy and what remained of the sack of hard bread aboard the boat. They had earlier stuffed their pockets and even the linings of their coats with hard bread.

"We are going to have to scull the boat because we have only one oar," said Donaldson.

"I know how to scull, did it in the Navy," said Neil.

"We should take the coats with us and hold them in the wind. They may be able to serve as a sail," said Donaldson.

"They won't be much good, we cut them up," said Neil.

In a few minutes, the jolly boat was in the water. Captain Maxwell had to be helped aboard. Neil was the last to get aboard. He pushed the boat off with the oar, put the oar in through the hole in the counter, and started sculling down wind towards Raleigh Cape, not knowing where they would end up.

It took two hours to make the trip to Raleigh Cape, with the help of the Captain's coat held high in the wind by Richard McFie and Charley Donaldson. When they went around the Cape the sea was still very high and there was a stiff breeze.

"I will try and put the boat in the gulch over there," Neil said, pointing to the place where he hoped to land everyone safely. The sea drove the jolly boat towards the land, sending it into the small gulch. McFie jumped out on the rocks, holding the painter to prevent the boat from going out with the sea. He secured the painter under a rock.

Maxwell was slow moving. He got near the side of the boat but didn't jump quickly enough. When he did jump, he went into the water between the boat and the cliff. He disappeared from sight as a wave rolled in, carrying him with it when it ebbed and flowed. Neil was unable to go to his assistance due to the condition of his knees, he could hardly stand, he was also the farthest from him. Maxwell went in under the boat and couldn't be seen.

"Look on the other side," Donaldson shouted to McFie, who jumped aboard the boat just as Maxwell came up. McFie grabbed him and tried to take him aboard.

"Give me a helping hand, Charley," he screamed.

Donaldson and McFie managed to pull Maxwell aboard. He was coughing, vomiting, and gasping for breath. Neil succeeded in pulling the boat close to the rocky shoreline and somehow jumped out.

McFie and Donaldson helped Maxwell ashore just as a large wave came in and turned the boat over, then carried it out to sea. What remained of the sack of hard bread and the keg of cherry brandy went with it.

The three men got Maxwell a little further up the cliff and laid him down on a soft bed of snow. It was soon evident he wasn't going to last very long. The rescuers sat on the rocks near him and tried to make him as comfortable as possible. They could see he was dying, his eyes were wide open and staring into space, his breathing was very slow. In less than ten minutes, he gave a deep shuddering sigh. Captain Maxwell was dead.

There were now only three of them left.

*****

Not far from where the Captain died there was a small rocky beach. Neil said they might get enough rocks there to cover his body. The other two nodded in agreement. Neil also noted that they should keep the Captain's pocket watch to give to his family.

They took off the heavy coat the Captain had put back on just before he fell into the water and folded it along with his cap. They might need both.

"The best thing to do is drag the body over to the rocks and pack the rocks on top. It's better than bringing the rocks over here," said Donaldson.

It didn't take them long to cover the Captain's body with rocks and bow their heads in a short prayer.

Soon afterwards, they were on their way to the top of the barren hill.

Their hope was to find the place called Quirpon.

Chapter 14

AN INDIAN NAMED JOSEPH

The trio of marooned men walked to the top of the cliff to get a better look at their surroundings. What they saw was wilderness. As far as the eye could see to the westward were inland lakes and forest. To the east was ocean with headlands jutting out into it.

"Which way should we go?" asked McFie.

"I don't know," said Donaldson, "Neil may have some idea."

"According to Jack Brown, the fishing village should be in a southerly direction next to a high mountain. He told us it was on an island somewhere and if that's the case it should be toward that high mountain in the distance." Neil pointed south toward the mountain.

"I wouldn't be in too big a hurry expecting to meet people out near the ocean. If anyone lives out there it's only during the summer. They would move inland in the fall to go trapping, hunting and cut firewood," said McFie.

"Look!" Neil pointed excitedly. "Do you see that mountain? That could be the one Jack was referring to, it's the highest one around."

After thinking about it and sizing things up they made a decision to go to the northwest for five or six miles to see what was there. If they didn't see anything in that direction, they would head south towards the mountain.

"It is impossible for me to travel with you right now," said Neil."I can hardly stand. I have to rest up for a while."

McFie nodded. "You stay here while we go inland and have a look. It won't take us long. You should be fine here. If it gets too cold, go down into the gulch, there's no wind down there. We'll check for you down there when we return."

As the duo left on their journey, Neil noticed they were both limping. He wondered how long they would last, and if indeed they would ever return. When he was alone, Neil started thinking about his situation. He knew he was in bad shape. His two feet had been frozen and were causing excruciating pain, so much that he could barely put them to the ground. Both of his hands had frozen too. Most of the skin on the backs of both of his hands was falling off. His two knees were skinned to the bone. His elbows were even worse than his knees. He was hungry and thirsty as well, but he knew he could battle that another while. The hard bread in his pocket could last for another day or so, as long as he could get his hands in his pockets to retrieve it.

As Neil sat on a rock and watched Donaldson and McFie slowly disappear from sight, he started thinking about the Captain and the Mate. "What does this all mean?" he mused. "Only a few days ago they were living it up aboard the *Rebecca*. Plenty of cooked food, lots to drink, and the women visiting them every night. They were living like kings and now they're dead."

Of the eleven people who had been in the Captain's quarters, Neil was the only one still alive. If the Captain had only listened to him, he thought with deep regret, they wouldn't have been in this mess.

It was cold where Neil was sitting, the northwest wind was piercing his bones. He looked around for a better place, but couldn't see anywhere close to the barrens. He looked at the Captain's watch and saw it was afternoon. He would have to make sure to keep the watch wound up.

Neil thought about the time he had spent in Jamaica's warm climate and what a fool he had been to join the *Rebecca*. But how could he have known? It wasn't the vessel, anyway, it was the men running the show!

His spirits low, Neil decided to go down into the gulch where the body of Captain Maxwell was covered with rocks and where he would be out of the wind.

* * * * *

McFie and Donaldson walked along by the barrens for a couple of miles then went into the woods and down towards a large pond. The ice on the pond was strong enough to hold them up. They walked southwest along the pond for nearly a mile, then turned to the right. There was a large bay or some other inlet this way. They walked for just about another mile to the running out of the pond, and entered the woods in a cut trail at the west end. There were numerous animal tracks along the trail. After walking for approximately a mile, they were excited to come upon human tracks. As they were about to go out from the thick woods near the shoreline, Donaldson stopped and looked at McFie.

"Do you smell smoke?" he asked.

McFie gave a few sniffs in the air. "Yes, I think I do," he said.

Donaldson was positive it was smoke. "Somebody must be around," he said.

"Which direction should we go?" McFie whispered as if the mystery person might hear them.

Donaldson checked the wind. He looked at McFie. "Richard," he asked. "Are you nervous?"

"No, only uneasy," said McFie.

"It has to be people, you know. Animals don't have fires burning."

The two men hadn't gone far when they saw a tilt at the edge of a cluster of trees. They hurried towards it. The tilt wasn't more than a few logs with a sharp roof on top. The roof was covered with birch bark shingles. There was a door that swung in. McFie called a greeting as they got within a hundred feet. Someone called back, but it wasn't from inside the cabin. The sound came from the woods. The two men went closer to the tilt and called again.

"Hello, can you hear me? We need help, help!" yelled McFie.

Suddenly a man stepped out from behind some trees not far away. "You need help," he said.

"Yes, we need help," said McFie.

The man walked toward them, he carried an axe, and had a rope over his shoulder. As he got closer they could tell he was a native, either a Newfoundland Indian or an Eskimo. They wondered if he understood English.

"We are shipwrecked near the shoreline," said McFie.

The man came closer and held up his hand. "You English?"

Surprised, they both answered, "Yes."

"Me speak English, name Joseph," he said.

"We lost ship, many drown," said Donaldson.

"Bad," said the man.

"We hungry, no food, feet and hands frozen," said McFie.

It was obvious this native had been in contact with white men since he wore leather boots and had pants made from cloth.

"You come in hut," he said.

Joseph went in followed by McFie and Donaldson. It was dark inside but to the two stranded sailors the tilt was like a palace. The fireplace burned brightly, giving off welcome heat six feet away. There was a strong smell of animal skins, likely beaver, as several were stacked near the wall. Hanging on a wire was an iron pot with steam coming from it, and what looked like some kind of stew inside. Donaldson was anxious to get some of whatever it was!

Joseph told them he was an Indian. He said he was part of an English crew with summer headquarters on Quirpon Island. During the fall, he packed supplies to last the winter and paddled his canoe to an area now called Pistolet Bay. He would trap there during the fall and most of the winter, then he would move to a winter tilt and spend the rest of the season making skin boots. In the spring, he would move to Quirpon and sell his furs to the French admirals, then he would go fishing for salmon with Isaac Isaacs.

He had learned to speak English from Isaac Isaacs, he said. Isaacs was an elderly Englishman who had a contract with the French Admirals to act as caretaker for the French fishing rooms between L'Anse aux Meadows and St. Lunaire. Isaacs had his headquarters on Quirpon Island.

Donaldson and McFie estimated Joseph to be approximately fifty. After talking to him for some time, it was clearly understood that the place they were looking for was Quirpon Island.

Joseph invited them to stay the night, saying it was late in the evening and a storm was approaching. They were happy to accept the invitation.

Donaldson and McFie ate the beaver stew Joseph had made and found it delicious; it was their first hot meal since leaving the *Rebecca*. Hunger, however, was not the greatest challenge facing the two Englishmen. They were in such agony with their feet that tears ran down their faces. They told Joseph they had frozen feet. He shook his head to indicate there was nothing he could do for them. That night, Donaldson could not sleep. He figured the heat from the fireplace was making his feet and hands more painful than if he was out in the cold.

At dawn, the storm was still raging and nothing could be seen. Joseph had left before daylight, saying he was going to check his traps.

"You stay, storm on all day," he told Donaldson, who relayed the message to McFie. They had no problem deciding to stay on.

* * * * *

Neil experienced a terrible night after the wind came around from the southeast. Seeking shelter, he bedded down in the gulch. He got the Captain's long black coat and, even though it was half frozen, he managed to wrap it around his legs. Around about midnight he heard loud howls that frightened him.

"Good grief, it's wolves, must be a whole pack of them! I hope they don't attack me," he murmured.

All night he heard the wolves, at times it seemed they were very close, at the top of the hill above him. He fumbled around in the snow and found a couple of small stones he thought he could use if the wolves attacked him. All night he waited in the shelter of the cliff as the blizzard raged. He was cold, hungry, wet, and his feet and hands hurt. To make things even worse, with wolves howling around him, he thought for sure he would be devoured at any minute!

As he huddled through the dark cold night, Neil was filled with the thought that he should have died with Captain Maxwell, who was resting a few feet away from him under a mound of rocks. He figured he would be better off dead than alive.

"Maybe the wolves have killed Charley and Richard. Maybe they're gone and I'm the only one left." Neil was downcast. Now he would have to do whatever had to be done alone. With those thoughts flitting through his mind, he lay down by the rocky cliff and drifted off to sleep.

He awoke as dawn was breaking. The wind was from the southeast with blowing snow. The sea was roaring as it rushed into the small cove; he knew the waves were high.

"I must have slept for most of the night and the wolves didn't get me," he said aloud.

Neil could hear some kind of odd noise as the sea rolled in. He knew something must be on the beach, but poor visibility kept him from seeing what it was. As he lay waiting for it to get lighter, he knew he would soon have to get moving. Maybe he could find the tracks of his companions and follow them. He had to find them or he was doomed.

With much pain involved, he plunged his hand into his coat pocket and retrieved a piece of hard bread. It was no longer that hard, having been soaked well in salt water. After he had consumed a few pieces of hard bread, his hunger pains subsided, but the burning in his feet and legs was killing him. On his hands, the area where the skin had come off was beginning to scab over. Any movement at all made the scabs crack and caused bleeding.

He removed the Captain's heavy coat from his legs and tried to stand up, but it was almost impossible. His feet hurt so much he could barely touch the ground. His knees and elbows were so sore he dared not brush them against anything.

Standing on his feet was his biggest problem, but he had to do it. He talked to himself, giving himself orders, commanding himself sternly to get up. He reached for the cliff hanging over his head and lifted himself up slowly and gingerly. He groaned in agony as he stood by the cliff and looked around the small rocky cove. He was about to start climbing the steep hill when he saw something on the beach and realized it was the jolly boat. As he stood and looked at the boat, he could see the damaged side. Without major repairs, it would be impossible to use it again.

Neil started climbing the hill. It was a slow and painful process. Blowing snow made visibility next to zero. He wondered if he would be able to follow the footprints of his two companions. At the top of the hill, he paused and looked around, but could not see very far. As he squinted, he was able to make out human tracks along the barrens and he started following them. He knew the direction Donaldson and McFie had taken because he'd watched them on their way for quite some time.

When he got into the valley, the tracks were covered in snow. But he kept going until he reached the pond, thinking he might once again pick them up. He had to stop and sit down at the pond; his feet were so painful that with every step it felt as though he was being stabbed with a knife. He pulled up his pants and looked at his lower legs. They were swollen tight in his boots, probably three times their normal size and red to the knees. He couldn't bear the touch of his fingers on the flesh above his boots.

As he sat there, he knew he had to continue on. The wind was in his back. It was only a matter of getting his feet moving. With all the determination he could muster, Neil got to his feet and headed for the pond. He had to find McFie and Donaldson.

* * * * *

In Joseph's tilt, McFie and Donaldson spent the day keeping the fire going. If it had not been for their painful feet and hands, they would have been quite comfortable.

Donaldson started to remove his boots, but he couldn't stand the pain. When McFie tried to help him by pulling on them he had to tell him to stop. Donaldson knew their chances of surviving this ordeal were slim. For one thing, he told McFie, even if they found the caretaker at the place called Quirpon, how was he going to treat their frozen feet and hands? What could he do?

They wondered about Neil and what he would do to survive. They knew he had no shelter and nothing to eat.

"He should have come with us regardless of the pain in his feet; he would have made it," said Donaldson.

"I'm not certain Neil even made it through the night," said

McFie. "It must have been very blustery on that shoreline with no shelter. You can be as tough as you like but there's only so much human flesh can stand."

"Maybe it's just the two of us left now," Donaldson looked sad.

"We don't know," said McFie. "When the storm is over we'll head back and see what happened to Neil."

During the late afternoon Joseph came back, carrying a load of skins and some meat he said was beaver.

"Weather not good," he said.

They made it clear to him that they wanted to stay another night. He nodded in agreement.

The storm kept up until daylight when it lightened a little.

"We have to go and see if we can find our friend. He needs us," Donaldson and McFie told Joseph.

"You come back with friend. I show you short way to Quirpon," he told them.

"In case we don't come back, would you be able to draw a map showing the way to Quirpon?" asked McFie.

"I draw map," said Joseph.

He got a piece of fox skin and used a sharp stick to scratch a map of the area. He also scratched the trail to get there as best he could. "You go toward sunrise. Get to Quirpon Island. High mountain," he said.

Donaldson thanked him as he rolled the skin map up and placed it inside his shirt.

After it got fully light, Donaldson and McFie ate more of the beaver stew and then they put on their dry clothes and departed. It was time to go back and find Neil.

* * * * *

Neil got halfway down the large pond. Visibility was zero. He couldn't see any human tracks. He wasn't even sure Donaldson and McFie had gone as far as this.

Neil went into the thick woods by the side of the pond and decided to stay there all night. He was in a partly sheltered area, away from the strife of the wind.

His hands were too sore to break off branches and make a shelter so he stamped out a place in the snow with his feet. It was under a tree for shelter. He was afraid to go calling to Donaldson and McFie for fear of attracting the wolves. As darkness crept in, so did the cold chilly night!

Sometime around midnight, Neil heard the howling of the wolves, the same as the night before, just more of them and closer. He didn't know what to do!

Not far from where he was bedded down, he saw a large birch tree. He would have to climb it. He knew it was his only hope. He saw a branch about six feet above the snow and somehow pulled himself up into the tree.

All night long the wolves howled and circled the tree. Sometime during the night, Neil realized his feet must have frozen again for the pain had gone. As daylight came, the wolves left, leaving tracks everywhere he looked.

After an hour or so waiting to see if the wolves would return, Neil agonizingly climbed down from the tree and made his way along the side of the pond. He fell in the deep snow several times and had great trouble getting up.

He had no idea where to find his two companions.

He was alone and fearful.

After walking for about an hour, he was exhausted and had no choice but to sit and rest a while.

"I suppose this is the place I'll die," he heard himself saying as he sat down in the snow. With those words, he fell asleep.

* * * * *

When they left Joseph's tilt, Donaldson and McFie walked back the way they'd come two days earlier. There were no tracks to follow, but they had an idea where to take the cut trail that led to the large pond in the back woods. By now, the snow was nearly knee-high. They were surprised to see so many wolf tracks along the trail leading to the pond. They also saw caribou tracks.

When they came to the pond and headed in an easterly direction, they saw human tracks in the snow. They were sure they belonged to Neil.

They started following the tracks. They saw where he had fallen several times, and realized he was in very bad shape. They travelled for a couple of miles more and there he was! They found him asleep at the edge of the pond. At first they thought he was dead. There was no movement as they approached.

"Hey, Neil," McFie called.

There was no movement so he called again.

Neil stirred. He'd heard something but didn't know what it was. The half starved, frightened, and very cold man nearly jumped out of his skin as he awoke. He thought the wolves were attacking him. He drew his knees up close to his chest and wrapped his arms around his head, waiting for their teeth to sink in. He began screaming.

"Neil, hey Neil, it's me, McFie."

For a moment Neil couldn't make any sense of what McFie was saying. He was half crazed, ready to strike at the closest thing that came near him.

"Just a moment, Richard," said Donaldson. "Step back and see what happens."

McFie stepped back and called again.

Neil finally recognized the voice. He took his arms from around his head.

"I thought you were wolves attacking me." His voice shook. "Thank God, oh thank God, you are Richard."

McFie caught Neil by the shoulders and helped him up. It was obvious he wasn't in his right mind. Neil asked who was the other man with McFie.

"Neil, it's me, Donaldson."

Neil stared at him.

"Charles," he said then. "I'm almost at my wit's end. I've had a rough two nights; the wolves were ready to attack me." Neil looked as though he had aged ten years in three days. "I'm so glad to see you two. I really thought the wolves might have devoured you by now."

Donaldson told him how they had found a tilt owned by an Indian named Joseph who had taken them in and given them food.

"We are taking you to the tilt, it's only a couple of miles from here," said McFie.

The three men started on their way. Neil, who could hardly stand, was helped along by Donaldson. They staggered slowly along, step by step, sometimes Donaldson and McFie were nearly carrying Neil. By the time they reached the tilt, it was after dark. Neil said he'd never seen anything in his life as beautiful as the tilt.

Joseph wasn't there.

Donaldson went inside and lit the lantern. The smoldering coals in the fireplace rekindled after McFie put a few shavings on them and blew under them. He added kindling, and soon had a blazing fire going. The pot of beaver stew still hung from the wire near the fireplace. Donaldson moved the pot over the fire to warm it up.

After the heat started circulating in the tilt, Neil's feet began to hurt. The pain was unbearable.

"We are going through the same thing as you," Donaldson said, as he saw Neil wince in pain. "It may be infection beginning to set in our feet."

"My hands are worse than my feet," said McFie. "Looks like a red streak going up my arm. If that's the case, it could be blood poisoning."

"I believe the same is happening to me," said Donaldson.

"Me too," said Neil.

The trio sat and stared at the floor, each one knowing what the other was thinking. They were all consumed with wondering what they were going to do. They knew they needed medical help and soon. Without it, their chances of survival were slim.

"I don't think I'll ever be able to leave this cabin again," said Neil.

"Don't worry, you'll leave when the time comes tomorrow morning," said McFie. "Donaldson has a map of the area that Joseph drew. A shortcut from the pond puts us closer to Quirpon."

The beaver stew was now warm, but the men waited for Joseph to arrive before they began eating. He didn't show up and they didn't know what to think.

"Something must have happened to him," said McFie. "The wolves may have got him."

"I'd say he's too smart for the wolves," said Donaldson.

They waited some more, but when Joseph still didn't appear they began to eat the stew. Neil thought it was the best meal he'd ever had in his life. Warm, and with a full stomach, he lay down on the mud floor and fell sleep.

McFie and Donaldson stayed awake for several hours, but when Joseph still didn't show up they lay down as well.

McFie was a light sleeper; he kept the fire going all night.

As daylight approached, they were awakened by the sound of someone at the door.

It was Joseph.

He seemed happy to see all of them.

They made it clear they needed medical attention for their feet and hands. He understood!

They asked him if he knew where to get help.

"Quirpon Island, Mr. Isaacs," he answered.

It was evident that they would have to get to Quirpon Island as soon as possible.

Before they left, Joseph gave them some dried fish to take with them. They thanked him for his kindness and bid him farewell.

Chapter 15

QUIRPON

It was the 26th of November when the three mariners set out on that cold frosty morning. The northwest wind had been blowing snow all night and the going was tough.

Each man found it hard to put his feet to the ground. Donaldson's feet were the worst, only God knew what it had taken to get him started. Although it was just two miles to the pond, it took them until noon to get that far. There were times when Donaldson wanted to return to the tilt and stay there, but Neil and McFie persuaded him to travel on.

They found a marked walking trail on the south side of the pond. Someone had used an axe to mark the trail. They could see a man's tracks on the trail, and the axe marks on the trees looked new, no more than a day or so old.

"This is the trail marked here," said Donaldson, holding up the map Joseph had drawn for them.

The three headed through a wooded area. They soon came across two round birch sticks, about four feet in length and two inches in diameter, leaning against a tree. They realized that Joseph, who had likely marked the trail, had put the sticks there for their use. They would make useful clubs to fight off wild animals.

"Those clubs are great weapons to fight off wolves." Neil was serious.

"I guess so," said Donaldson, as he picked one up.

"It looks like Joseph blazed this trail for us yesterday," said Donaldson. "He's a good man. He wants to help us."

"He has helped us a lot already," said McFie.

The three men hadn't gone far when they came to a large marshy area. They could see the high mountain in the distance.

"That's the mountain Joseph was talking about yesterday," said Donaldson. "But it's a long way from here."

"It's getting late, we should go into the woods and stay for the night," said McFie. "A fire would be nice... I would have taken a flint and steel to make a fire if there had been extra ones at the tilt. But I saw only one flint and steel in Joseph's tinderbox and I certainly couldn't take that. And did you notice the jar full of what looked like dried goose down? I expect he uses that as tender to light a fire. I guess them Indians know what's best."

The men broke off tree boughs and put them on the ground. Their hands were bleeding even before they began this task. McFie suggested they should use the clubs Joseph had left them to break off boughs. After they had beaten off enough boughs, they piled them in a heap and huddled together, back on, to keep warm. During the night, they experienced cold temperatures with wind and drifting snow. Well before midnight, Donaldson informed his companions his two feet were frozen.

"They don't hurt anymore, there's no life in them, they must be frozen," he said in despair.

"My feet are the same," said McFie.

Neil was having pain in his feet, an indication they were not yet frozen.

Shortly before midnight they heard wolves howling; they seemed to be on the trail towards the pond. They made up their minds if they were attacked they would fight the wolves off with the birch clubs.

During the night they talked about the man Joseph called Isaac Isaacs, speculating he must be the person in charge in the area, like an Admiral or a Governor.

"I don't know who he is," said Neil. "All I hope is that he's familiar with frozen feet and hands and can do something to help all of us."

"If only we can reach him in time," said McFie.

"We don't know how far it is or where we have to go, only toward the sun, which is east," said Donaldson.

"Suppose the weather comes bad and we can't see anything, what will we do then?" asked McFie.

"If that happens, we will have to hold up somewhere until the storm is over," said Neil.

"We have to keep going when it's daylight. We have to keep on as long as we can see," said Donaldson.

About an hour before daylight it was very cold. The wind had died down. The stars above were twinkling brightly and the only sound was an occasional howl from some hungry, lonely animal.

Neil didn't say anything, but he knew his two feet were frozen from the tops of his boots down, there was no life in them.

Daylight found them on their way. They were soon out of the woods and walking arm in arm as best they could across the open bogs. The glow of the sun was in their eyes as it peeked over the horizon.

"It looks as if it's going to be a good day, we should travel a long distance if we don't delay too long taking spells," said Neil. "We haven't got time to rest."

"To tell the truth, I don't know how I'm going to make it." Donaldson knew he was going to have a rough day. He wondered when he was going to have to say he gave up or order his companions to go on and leave him. But, no, that wasn't going to happen. He was bound and determined to go on until he dropped.

"You have to make it, even if we have to drag you," Neil told him. Donaldson nodded.

They walked across bogs bare of snow, blown away by the wind. Much to their surprise, they saw a lot of berries. McFie said they were the fruit of the rowan tree. Donaldson had also heard them called marsh berries.

They sat down and started picking the frozen berries, holding them in their hands until they had thawed enough to eat. The three of them were having serious problems with the backs of their hands; they were so sore and scabbed over that just moving them caused the scabs to crack open and bleed.

During the afternoon they came to open water, a bay. As they walked along the bottom of the bay, the temperature went up a little and their feet began to thaw out; this caused excruciating pain. Neil said they had to keep going as long as possible.

"I am ready to drop any moment," said Donaldson.

"We will have to go to the west in order to get around this bay, maybe somewhere to the south is Quirpon," said McFie.

They struggled on, arm in arm, along the frozen beach. They saw flocks of birds, eider ducks. The bay they were going around was known as Island Bay.

"If only we had a muzzle loader, there would be plenty of food," said McFie. After saying that, he fell into silence.

It was hard walking along the rocky beach and McFie decided to walk along the shoreline close by the edge of the high water mark. As he went along, he discovered partridge berry beds.

"Hey, come and have a look at these berries, you can almost shovel them up," he called.

Neil and Donaldson could hardly believe their eyes! You couldn't step anywhere without trampling on the berries. They decided to rip part of the lining from one of their long coats and shape a bag large enough to hold about two gallons of berries.

For the next few days, at least, they would feast on hard bread and partridge berries and perhaps some of the fish Joseph had given them.

They walked on for about another mile and then Donaldson said he had to rest. He said his feet could no longer carry his weight, they were too tender. As it was almost sundown, they decided to find a good place to stay the night.

The place they chose was not far from the water. The windswept trees that grew there had huge thick branches with a wide spread that would provide good cover for the night. Neil used the birch clubs to break off pieces of brush that he spread on the ground under the spruce canopy. He helped Donaldson over to lie down.

"McFie and I are going to take a look around and see if there are any signs of human habitation," Neil said.

Donaldson was satisfied to lie on the bed of boughs. He mumbled to himself, "I've had it." He couldn't see how he could continue any further.

Neil and McFie walked around a cove in the inner part of the bay until they came to a brook. They decided to walk up along the brook and see if there was a place to get across where the water wasn't too deep. They hadn't walked far when they came to a spot where the brook widened. It looked as though they could cross there without too much difficulty.

They talked about Donaldson and agreed he was a very sick man. His temperature was up, and McFie said Donaldson had pulled up his pants and showed him his leg. There was a red streak going up his leg, a sure sign of infection.

Neil was very concerned. "Donaldson is only thirty. He's a strong, well built Englishman who could do any kind of job aboard the *Rebecca* and now he is doomed. A man can't live without his feet."

The three stranded men had a miserable night huddled together underneath the spruce tree. Donaldson groaned most of the night; the little sleep he got was broken by nightmares about the loss of the *Rebecca*.

When the dawning broke, the sun came up in a blaze of red, casting what seemed the shadows of hell over the three wandering souls who were looking for something they thought might never have existed.

This was the third day since leaving Joseph's tilt.

Where they were heading they didn't know. All they knew was what Joseph had told them and all they had was the map he'd drawn for them on part of a fox skin. For all they knew, Isaac Isaacs might be away somewhere in the forest or gone back to England. He might not be at Quirpon at all. Joseph might have made up the story about him to get them away from his trap lines. No, that couldn't be true. It wasn't true. They had the map and the name Isaac Isaacs, all things that kept their hopes alive.

Neil looked at Donaldson, who didn't look at all well, and said he had to get on his feet, it was time to move.

Donaldson was not faint-hearted. During the night, he had made up his mind to keep going. As long as his two companions could stand on their feet, he would too. Saying he would give him a hand, Neil took his hand and shoulder and lifted him to his feet. He staggered a little but caught himself on a nearby tree. Neil also helped McFie to his feet.

"We should be able to get a fine distance today, if the weather remains good and our feet hold out." Neil tried to sound encouraging and hopeful. "After we get across the brook, we may have better going on the other side."

McFie was shivering and it seemed as though he would fall. Neil caught him by the arm and steadied him.

"You'll be all right after you get on the move," he told him. "We are all finding it difficult this morning."

"I think I'd rather die than start walking in this God forsaken place this morning." McFie groaned loudly as his feet touched the ground. "Especially when I'm heading to nowhere."

Neil didn't comment.

They crossed the brook without much difficulty and proceeded along the shoreline. After they rounded a bend, they found themselves on a sandy beach. They kept below the high water mark because it was softer underfoot. There wasn't any snow on the beach and the tide was out.

They walked close to each other as they slowly trod along, limping, stopping, and moving on again. This pattern continued all morning as they followed the shoreline, in and out of small coves. A few times, they attempted to walk across the narrow point that would have made the distance shorter but brush, about three feet high, made the going too rough for their feet. Following the shoreline made for a much longer trip around Island Bay. In mid-afternoon, they decided to stop; they couldn't endure the pain in their feet and legs any longer.

"I suppose this is where we'll die, somewhere along this beach." McFie sounded resigned to his fate.

"I won't be dying along this beach as long as I can move one toe." Donaldson spoke with determination. "The only thing that will stop me is getting tore up by some wild beast."

"Keep your courage up, McFie," said Neil. "Under that high mountain over there is Quirpon. Once we get there we can take off our boots and have someone look at our feet."

"I'm afraid for someone to look at my feet," said Donaldson. "With all the pain I'm having I would say they are rotten bags of pus."

The men sat down on a ledge not far from the high water mark and looked out over the bay. There were a lot of small islands everywhere.

"I would say there are about a million birds in this bay. This must be the best hunting place in the world," said Neil.

"Yes, and we are here without a shotgun, starving to death," said Donaldson.

McFie pulled up his pants and showed his companions his legs; they were swollen tight in his boots with red streaks going up them.

"I know that the red streaks are a sign infection is setting in." McFie said matter of factly. "Every time I put my foot to the ground the pain almost kills me."

"I know," said Neil, looking up at the sky. "But we can't go any further... we are going to have to stay here all night, looks to me like there's weather coming on."

"We should go around the next bend before we stop," said Donaldson. "We might be able to find a place there to spend the night. I'll go and take a look."

He walked a short distance and noticed a large bog. Wondering where it led, he walked out into the middle. He saw water on the other side of the bog and figured it would be a shortcut if they went that way. The going on the bog wasn't as bad as on the beach, and Donaldson thought McFie would be able to manage it. When he returned, McFie was asleep and he told Neil what he had found.

"We can make up some lost time if we cross the bog just ahead. We should keep going, supposing we have to carry McFie. What do you think of him anyway?" he said.

"I'm afraid for him," Neil said. "Blood poisoning is dangerous. It can kill you if it's not treated."

He and Donaldson got McFie on the move and he limped along as best he could. The trio moved across the bog and out on the shoreline again. By now Neil was moving slowly, but he continued to help McFie as much as possible. After a while, Neil stopped and said they had to start looking for a place to stay the night right away.

"I think the wind is going to come around from the northwest; the clouds are starting to move in this direction. I will go on ahead and see if I can find a place where we can spend the night," he said to Donaldson. "You help McFie to keep moving."

Donaldson caught McFie's arm as Neil went on ahead to scout out the area. After about a mile, Neil found a deep cove where a spot of large trees stood. It was obvious to him that someone had been cutting there a couple of years ago. To a man stranded in the wilderness, it was a sign of hope that someone had been there.

He found a place of shelter in heavy brush he figured would protect them from a northwest gale and began beating off branches with the birch stick he had been carrying all day. The branches were spruce and hard to break. The backs of his hands hurt and bled every time he swung the stick, but he kept on until he had enough branches for them to lie on. As he looked around he saw the high mountain. He knew in his heart they were slowly getting closer to the place called Quirpon.

Neil walked back to meet his two comrades. They were on a long straight shoreline with rocky outcrops and when he met them they were sitting on the shoreline, looking completely exhausted.

"There's a good place to spend the night not far from here. It's in a sheltered cove," Neil told them. "If we can keep going for another half hour we can get to it."

"We'll make it." Donaldson's voice was firm and steady. "You go on ahead and beat off a few branches to lie down on. We'll take our time getting there."

"I've already got enough branches ready for the three of us to lie down on. Let's go on."

It was after dark by the time they reached their destination and got ready to bed down for the night. Donaldson had the bag with the berries in it tied to the back of his coat. They pulled the bag open and found that most of the berries were squashed. There were enough, however, to make their stomachs feel a little better.

Sometime during the night the wind picked up and it started snowing.

"We are in a very good place here. It's too bad we don't have something to go over us and keep us from getting wet," said Neil.

"Can't we beat off more boughs and put them on top of us?" Donaldson asked.

"I'm not going to attempt it in the dark," said Neil. "I am afraid I may strike the back of my hands or hit my feet. It would kill me if that happened."

It was a very dark night, no stars were shining. During the night, they heard many strange animal sounds, some coming from the ocean. The sounds were ones none of them had ever heard before.

"Must be seals of some kind, it sure isn't wolves" said McFie.

"Maybe here in the New World there are animals that crawl upon the land at night and devour everything, especially people," Neil was half serious.

"God grant it." Donaldson wasn't joking. "We could then be out of our punishment."

"I know of a better way to die than to be eaten by some monster crawling in from the briny ocean," said Neil.

"Listen boys, if we saw a monster coming through the woods we would all die with fright, so don't worry about it," McFie had the last word on the subject.

All night they lay waiting and wondering what was going to happen the following day. The next morning was very cold. They all knew their feet had frozen during the night because there was no pain, only a feeling of numbness. Neil was the first to rise; he had spent the night next to the large spruce tree. His hands were burning as though they were in a fire and his palms were swollen to the point he could not close them. Neither of them had slept during the night, for hours they said nothing, just groaned in pain.

Neil thought about his mother back home. If the three of them died here in this wilderness no one would ever know what had become of them. Joseph would not be able to explain to the mysterious Isaacs what had happened to the *Rebecca* or to them. They would end up in the New World unknown, their bones bleached in the sands of time.

Neil thought about those things and resolved that he had to survive. He had to get to the place called Quirpon.

* * * * *

Just after dawn, the three got underway again.

Walking was a little better, the pain they had wasn't as severe as it had been the evening before simply because their feet were frozen and numb. It was high tide so they moved off the beach and soon came to a grassy meadow-like area. It looked strange.

"Someone has been here before. Nature did not do this. It looks like an enclosed compound," said Donaldson, noticing places where buildings used to be. (The men did not know, and would never know, that they were standing where the Vikings had once had a settlement in L'Anse aux Meadows.)

"Someone might have been here but there's no one here now and that's for sure," said McFie.

They continued on but found nothing, no signs of life.

By this time, they were all in great pain.

"We'll have to stop for a while. I can't put my feet to the ground any more." Donaldson sat on a ledge and looked out over the sea. He was struck by the beauty of the place even though he was suffering. From where he was sitting he could see the outline of a high hill to their left.

"Do you think that's the mountain we are looking for, near Quirpon?" he asked.

"No, that's not the mountain," said Neil. "The one we are looking for is much further along, probably six or eight miles further south. I was looking at that hill yesterday, that's not it," he paused. "We haven't come very far today, about two or three miles, we have to keep going at all costs."

Neil tried to encourage the other two even though every step he took made him cringe in pain. Donaldson agreed they would have to go on.

From where they were sitting, Neil knew it wasn't much use going further out on the point of land. They would have to go in a southerly direction in order to get to Quirpon. They started walking across the open hills. In several places, they saw what looked like old footpaths, and rocks piled in straight lines at perfect ninety degree angles. After a couple of hours of dragging one another along, they came to an area where the shoreline sloped away to smooth slippery rock.

Neil was walking ahead and didn't notice the slippery conditions he was stepping on. Without any warning, his footing gave way and he fell! He slid down over the rocky shoreline and landed on the beach about ten feet below. He lay there for a few minutes, face down and semi-conscious, and wondering what he'd done to himself.

He rolled over then and sat up. He looked at his left hand, it was bleeding badly, the scabs were torn off with the flesh, there was bare skin right to the bone, and his right elbow felt as though it was smashed. He heard Donaldson calling him, but he was unable to answer.

After a few minutes, he was finally able to get to his feet and call back to his companions.

"Stay where you are. I'll be up in a few minutes." He walked around the cliff and came back up. He was badly shaken.

"We thought it was the end of you when we saw you go out of sight," said McFie.

When he and Donaldson saw the condition of his hand they realized Neil had a serious injury. He said he thought his fingers were broken, at least they felt like they were, and he said he knew his elbow was smashed.

Donaldson examined him. Neil's elbow wasn't broken, the bones were intact but the flesh was torn off again.

"We'll have to tear off another strip of your coat to bandage your hand and elbow and try to stop the bleeding." Donaldson bandaged Neil's hand and elbow as best he could.

"Let's stop for the night, it looks like a good place over there." McFie pointed to an indraft in a cliff not far away.

They did as he suggested and spent another very uncomfortable night trying to stay alive.

As daylight came, Neil could not get to his feet.

They ate some of the dried fish Joseph had given then. They also opened the sack of mashed partridge berries and ate them but it did very little for their hunger.

Neil noticed they were losing a lot of weight, he felt as though he was a bag of bones, his stomach had collapsed.

Both his hands were useless, swollen so much he couldn't close them. Holding on to anything was out of the question. He felt he would not last much longer without medical attention. The question was where was he going to get it.

If they found Isaac Isaacs he may not have anything to treat frozen feet or infection and what would he be able to do about broken bones?

Neil closed his eyes in the darkness. No matter what Isaac Isaacs didn't have, for sure he would have a warm stove and food and maybe something to cover them at night. With that thought, his faith grew stronger.

Donaldson struggled to his feet and helped the other two men to stand. He said he would go to the top of the hill and have a look.

"From what I saw yesterday it appears we may have to go south from here," said Neil. "Leave the shoreline and go inside the high hill to our right. It looks like a valley leading to the south."

Donaldson left and he somehow got to the top of a lookout and sat down. He could see a fair distance, flat barren country lay ahead. There were small ponds and bogs scattered everywhere. However, it looked like very good walking toward the south. As he sat and looked at the barrens in the distance, he saw something move! He knew it was animals of some kind. He stared as hard as he could. He could not remember seeing animals like that before. Coming back, he met Neil and McFie, who had managed to get to the top of the hill. He told them he'd seen a dozen or more large animals.

"It must be caribou," said Neil.

"Yes, it probably is. They are feeding around a barren not far from the top of the hill."

"If we had a musket, we would shoot one. We would have lots to eat then," said McFie.

Donaldson put his arm around Neil's shoulder and helped him scale the hill. Neil moaned in pain with every step. The three men watched the caribou feeding some distance away and all they could think was if only they had a gun. Not having one, all they could do was walk away. They could only manage a short distance before they had to stop; their feet were hurting so much. Around noon, they could see the valley going down into Noddy Bay. They forced themselves across the barrens and finally started descending. In the distance they saw a small pond in the valley, with a brook running from it out into the bay.

As they looked down the valley they could see the high mountain on Quirpon Island. They were much closer than they thought. They realized if all went well they should be in Quirpon the following day.

They had no problem finding a place to camp for the night. The tree cover was dense along the side of the hills, much too dense for snow to get under. They crawled in under and lay down on dry grass. They had shelter but they were still cold, wet and hungry.

During the night it became very cold from a northwest wind. Neil's condition was deteriorating. His injured hand was paining severely. He also had a pain under his arm and in his groin. He knew what those symptoms meant – lockjaw, a form of tetanus causing rigid closure of the jaws. If he came down with lockjaw he knew he'd be finished for sure. He didn't tell Donaldson or McFie for fear of causing panic.

Donaldson now seemed to be in the best condition. Although his left hand was badly infected, he could use it. His right hand was good, except for his little finger which was swollen and had turned dark. His feet were in bad condition, but his determination kept him pushing on.

Neil had to be dragged out from under the brush. He could not use his hands to crawl and his knees were sore and tender. McFie was equally as bad and said there was no way he could stand, let alone walk.

"You have to start walking," said Donaldson. "We have almost reached Quirpon. If we keep going we should be there around noon."

"I am unable to move." McFie looked grim. "Go on and leave me. I am going to die anyway."

"You won't die," said Donaldson.

"Come on, Richard, don't give up, keep going for one more day," said Neil.

Donaldson helped them both out from under the bushes. He somehow got them standing up and ordered them to start moving.

"I don't know if I will be able to move or not. I think I'm going to faint," said McFie.

Donaldson got a handful of snow and put it on McFie's forehead. In a minute or so, McFie regained his composure and settled down. Neil somehow took the birch stick he had been carrying in his right hand and used it as a crutch. It helped him tremendously, although the backs of his hands were cracked and bleeding.

The men moved steadily along, but almost at a snail's pace. Donaldson was holding McFie's arm while Neil hobbled in the rear with his crutch. They went for about a mile, then came to a long sandy beach at the bottom of a deep cove. They stopped for a few minutes and rested on the edge of the shoreline. They saw what they thought were walruses on the beach.

Donaldson got out the fox skin map Joseph had drawn and unfolded it. He knew Quirpon Island was somewhere south or east of where they were sitting.

"If the visibility was better we might be able to get the right direction to Quirpon, but I think we have to go around the cove and over the hill on the far side." He pointed to the high hill further east then south.

"The snow is up over my boots," said McFie. "My feet are wet again."

"In some places the snow is over two feet deep," said Donaldson. "But when we get up on the hill over there we should be able to see if there are any buildings around the harbour. According to our map we should only have a couple more miles to go."

To avoid the snow the men stayed on the beach and walked in the sand a little below the high water mark. Neil hobbled behind, he was in great trouble. At the end of the beach Donaldson waited for Neil to catch up.

"We will take our time going up the hill, it may be difficult picking our way through the brush. There are a couple of leads going up from here. We may be able to follow them," said Donaldson.

They started up the hill with Donaldson leading. It was a hard trek, Donaldson and McFie made the distance of half a mile in two hours; Neil lagged behind in their tracks.

Donaldson went back and met Neil slowly pushing his way through the snow. Every time he put his feet out to make a step he would cry out in pain. Donaldson helped him the rest of the way to the top.

They couldn't see far due to poor visibility, but they looked at the map again and agreed it wasn't completely accurate. It was simply an outline to get to the general area.

"Instead of us going to our right or left, we should go straight ahead to what appears to be another hill. When we get there, we can decide which way to go," said Neil.

Agreeing with Neil, they went down over the hill, crossed a valley and went up another hill. The weather was clearing as they reached the top. They sat down on the barren hill top, totally exhausted.

"According to the map, Quirpon Harbour is below us," Neil pointed at the map.

"Look," said McFie with excitement in his voice. "A man!"

"Where?" Neil and Donaldson asked at the same time.

"Over there on the other side... and a house," he pointed.

They looked. Sure enough, a man came out of a house and was walking towards a shed about a hundred feet away.

"Start shouting, start calling," Neil was almost beside himself.

Donaldson stood up and yelled frantically. The man kept walking, he didn't hear them.

Neil, Donaldson and McFie were so excited they forgot their dreadful condition for a few minutes. They knew now there were people at Quirpon Harbour. How could they attract their attention?

They stared across the harbour, looking closely at the area where the house stood. To their surprise they saw other buildings near the water as well as a wharf. They knew then this had to be the fishing premises belonging to the French. This was a place later called Grandmother's Cove.

They started waving frantically, anything to get the man's attention. But he was oblivious to them. The three of them wondered what could be done to let the people know they were there and needed help. Neil was scanning the shoreline, attempting to find something to cross over, when suddenly he saw a boat near the tickle.

"Look, a boat, a white boat near a shack on this side," he pointed to the area near the narrows.

"We have to get down there right away," said Donaldson, already starting to move in that direction.

"Just a moment, we have to look for the best route off this hill, there's a lot of brush around," said Neil.

The men did a quick survey and decided to move along the hill to the west and then down to the bottom of the cove. It looked to be more than a mile to the boat.

For the first time since leaving the wreck of the *Rebecca*, the three stranded sailors felt a real sense of optimism. After coming down the steep hill, sliding most of the way in the snow, they started walking around a cove, and then up over an enbankment to a flat bog. While walking along the bog, they came upon a trail in the snow. It had been made by a dog team pulling a sled.

"Those tracks were made today," Neil leaned over to take a close look.

The three were filled with excitement.

"I wonder which way they went?" said McFie.

Neil examined the dog prints. "They went inland. We'll use their trail and head for the boat."

The three men started hobbling at a faster pace along the trail towards the shack near the narrows, almost crying with pain as they walked. As they came over a small hill not far from the shoreline they could see the shack nearby. Then, to their surprise, they saw four large dogs looking their way and sniffing the air.

"Are you afraid of dogs, Neil?" asked Donaldson.

"At this moment, I am not afraid of the devil himself."

"No more am I," said McFie.

"Well, you two go ahead, I'll hang behind," said Donaldson.

As they got closer, the dogs started barking furiously and running toward them. Neil led the way with the birch stick, he wasn't afraid. A man came out of the shack to see what was going on. He began calling the dogs as they drew closer to Neil. The man called the dogs again and they stopped and retreated. Just then, the man saw them.

The man stood and looked their way for a minute, then ran back to the shack followed by the dogs. The man went inside and came out with another man. This time, they both had muskets in their hands.

The two men stood with legs apart, surrounded by the four savage dogs with teeth exposed as they growled at the three stranded sailors. The two men with muskets challenged the sailors as they got closer. Finally, Neil held up his hand for Donaldson and McFie to stop. The dogs came around them, barking furiously. The men with muskets said something to the dogs in a language Neil didn't understand.

"Do you speak English?" he asked.

"Yes, we speak English," one man said.

"We got shipwrecked along the coast many miles away and we need help. Our feet and hands are frozen."

Neil held out his hands to show them. The oldest of the two men looked at his hands and cringed; he could not believe what he was seeing. The men put their guns away and called the dogs.

"We Indians work for Mr. Isaacs," said one of the men.

"We're glad to see you. Do you have food? We are hungry." Neil pointed at himself and his two companions.

"Food, not much here, lots over there," the Indian said, gesturing to someplace on the island.

"Good," said Neil.

"You come inside," the other one said.

Neil, Donaldson, and McFie were delighted to go into the shack with the two Indians. Inside, there was a work bench along one side for repairing and making dog sleds, and tools for repairing boats were hung on the wall. There was an iron stove in one corner and a table with tin mugs hanging over it nearby. Steam was coming from an iron kettle sitting on top of the stove.

As they talked, they heard dogs barking.

"Sam coming," said one of the Indians.

The Indians went outside and called their dogs.

As an approaching dog team got closer, Neil could hear men yelling at the dogs and calling to the Indians, inquiring if they had seen anyone.

"Three men inside house," one Indian exclaimed.

Almost before the dog team stopped, a man entered the shed; he was wearing a seal skin coat and a fur hat.

"Who are these strangers?" he shouted.

"They shipwrecked men, walked here," said an apparently frightened Indian.

"I know they walked here, I saw their tracks," said the man, talking in a loud voice and looking straight at Neil.

"We went on the rocks near Cape Norman, we're the only survivors," said Neil.

The man could not see very well after coming in from the brightness of the snow. He shaded his eyes with his hand. "I saw your tracks where you came upon our trail coming around the cove. We knew it wasn't the Indians." The man lowered his voice.

"We're in terrible shape, had our feet and hands frozen and haven't eaten for many days," said Neil.

The man removed his cap. He had red hair and a very scruffy beard.

"Do you all speak English?" he asked.

"Yes, we're from England."

As the man's eyes adjusted to the dullness inside the shed, he again stared at Neil, who was sitting on a stool near the table, holding his bandaged left hand and doing the talking.

"Are you injured?" the man asked.

"Yes, we are all injured, our feet and hands are frozen. I think my elbow is broken and my knees are ripped apart." Neil spoke matter of factly.

"There's nothing we can do here. Mr. Isaacs is the person to help you with anything like this."

"My name is Neil Dewar, this is Charley Donaldson and Richard McFie."

"My name is Sam Lang. I'm from the east coast of England."

"We haven't eaten anything in days. It's been fourteen days since our ship went on the rocks, and about all we've had since then is a little hard bread and berries we picked in the snow," said Neil.

"We can give you a cup of tea and soft bread with roasted fish," Sam told them.

"We will be more than glad to get it, Sam, and we thank you very much," said Neil.

Neil was sitting not far from the stove and the pain in his feet and legs was driving him out of his mind. His boots were tight on his feet and he could barely touch his feet to the floor. He supposed the heat from the stove was making everything worse.

Not far from the building they were in there was a large dog pen. The other man who had just arrived penned the dogs in and came inside. Sam introduced him as Karl, a young Dutchman, twenty years old, who had jumped ship from a French man-of-war. He had served in the French Navy for two years and would have been captured and shot by a shore patrol if not for the connections between Isaac Isaacs and the French Admiral. The Admiral traded the young man to Isaacs' onshore crew for six carcasses of caribou.

Sam wasn't happy about taking the three stranded sailors across to the island. He told them this would be heaping extra trouble on Mr. Isaacs, and he was sure he would not like it.

"I'll have to go and see Mr. Isaacs before you go across to the island. I need his permission first," Sam said.

"You don't need his permission, Sam," the young Dutchman said. "These men are in bad shape. What are you going to do? Leave them here to die?"

"You never mind, young fellow. We can't take in every person who comes along. In no time at all we'll have all our food gone. Mr. Isaacs might not like it."

"Like it or not, Sam, when our boat goes across to the Island the three men will be in it." The Dutchman spoke with determination and seemed ready to punch Sam if he objected.

"Okay, okay, we'll take them across, but you'll take the responsibility for doing it," said Sam.

"I'm capable of taking the responsibility, don't worry."

Although he seemed uneasy about what Mr. Isaacs might say, Sam told Karl to get the boat launched and ready for their trip across the tickle.

The young Dutchman spoke very good English. He offered the sailors his lunch.

"You can eat while I help launch the boat and get it ready for the trip across," he said.

"Don't mind Karl," Sam said when the Dutchman had gone outside. "He doesn't care for anything, thinks he's still in Europe."

"We don't want to get you in any trouble, Sam, but we need help and there's no one else around," said Donaldson.

"It's not that I wouldn't take you across to our place. It's that I don't want to get across the grain with Mr. Isaacs."

"Don't worry about anything, Sam. Our company will pay for any costs we incur," said Neil.

"Okay, I'll tell Mr. Isaacs that."

Sam poured tea into three tin mugs, it was spruce tea, made from spruce buds steeped out. He emptied Karl's pack sack on the table and inside there was bread and roasted dry cod fish. To the three hungry survivors it was a feast. Neil could eat with his right hand; his left was bandaged with black cloth and swollen to twice its size.

Sam did not appear to pity them. He scarcely noticed the blood oozing from the scabs on their hands and the way they squirmed every time their feet touched the floor. Sam only wanted to know if they had seen any caribou on their route, how many there were, and where they saw them.

Karl suddenly appeared in the doorway and told Sam the boat was in the water. "We are ready to cross over when you are."

"Have you fed the dogs?" asked Sam.

"Yes, we have taken care of the dogs and scraped the whale bones of the sled and got everything secured."

"Okay, everyone aboard," said Sam.

Neil tried to walk but found it impossible.

Donaldson offered to help him, but as hard as he tried he could not get Neil to take the weight of his body on his feet. He slumped to the floor every time he tried.

It was roughly two hundred feet to the boat.

"We'll have to carry you," said Donaldson.

"Just a moment." Karl went and got the sled he had stuck up by the shed. "We'll use this to pull you to the boat."

He and Donaldson put Neil on the sled and got him aboard the boat. McFie hobbled along behind.

"We will have to take the sled with us. He's not capable of walking all the way to the house so we'll have to pull him," Karl directed his words at Sam.

"If we do that we will have to make two trips across. This boat won't handle everyone and the sled in one trip," said Sam.

Donaldson stayed back with the two Indians while the others crossed over. There wasn't much room to land on the other side. The harbour was frozen over and that meant a long walk to Grandmother's Cove.

Karl and Sam unloaded the sled. Sam then returned for the others, while Karl got Neil and McFie aboard the sled and said he would pull them. He said the going was very good. With two of the survivors seated on the sled, Karl headed towards Isaac Isaacs.

Chapter 16
MEETING ISAAC ISAACS

Isaac Isaacs came from the southeast of England near Dover. He had spent years sailing in the Royal Navy. He was fifty-eight years old and had never married and referred to himself as the first Newfoundlander. Isaacs came to Newfoundland as a guardian employed by the British government to prohibit foreigners from settling permanently in the colony. However, he later befriended French Admirals and secured a contract with them to guard their property after the fishing season was over and most everyone had left. The French supplied enough food to last him and his workers all winter, and paid his workers as guards. Besides mending French nets, Isaacs and his workers trapped and hunted during the winter and sold their furs come spring.

Isaac Isaacs was a tough customer, both feared and respected. He could work twenty-four hours for days on end without sleep. It was said he was prepared to meet any challenge regardless of the outcome. The French Admirals liked him because he was trustworthy. They valued him because without him all their fishing premises and gear would be gone, destroyed. He was honest, fearless and dependable. Isaacs also claimed to know a lot about medical treatment from his training in the British Navy.

Karl stopped as he approached the house of Isaac Isaacs and shouted very loudly several times. Isaacs had told his men to never approach the premises without giving a warning first.

"That's a good way to get shot," he would say.

Karl got no reply so he shouted again and this time he noticed movement near a shed by the shoreline.

"Mr. Isaacs, Mr. Isaacs," Karl yelled.

Isaacs came out of the shed and waved to them. Karl pulled the sled closer. Isaacs did not pay much attention to Karl until he saw the men on the sled. He immediately sensed something was wrong and held up his hand for Karl to stop.

"Has someone had an accident with a musket?" he asked in a loud voice.

"No, sir. We found three shipwrecked men from the British ship *Rebecca*. They are in poor condition," Karl replied loudly.

Isaacs said nothing for a minute and then he waved again to Karl.

"For God's sake,"he yelled. "Get the men inside the house."

Karl pulled the sled to the front door of the house and waited for Isaacs to walk from the shed. Isaacs was a tall man with a long white beard; the heavy dark coat he wore made him look much bigger then he really was.

McFie rolled off the sled and got to his feet with help from Karl.

"We can't shake hands with you, Mr. Isaacs, because our hands are too sore, we've had them frozen," McFie sounded apologetic.

Isaacs looked at the two men with horror. He noticed the terrible condition the backs of their hands were in and shuddered.

"Where did you get shipwrecked?" he asked.

"Cape Norman, sir, or on the point of land next to it," said Neil.

"This man can't stand on his feet, his two feet have been frozen several times." Karl pointed at Neil.

Isaacs and Karl helped Neil from the sled and carried him inside the house. McFic hobbled behind.

"You said there were three," said Isaacs.

"Sam is bringing the other man over," said Karl.

"Tell Sam to bring the dogs over too. We are going to have to move down to L' Anse au Pigeon. The house there is bigger and better for all of us," said Isaacs.

Inside the house, Isaacs lit the oil lamps and invited his guests to take off their heavy coats and sweaters. That was impossible. Their fingers were too sore to unbutton their coats. Isaacs had to remove them.

There was a large partly closed off fireplace at one end of the house. Isaacs opened the front of the fireplace and put two pieces of wood in. Neil and McFie sat in silence and stared at the fire, hardly able to believe they were safe and sound and under a roof.

"We are very happy to find you here, Mr. Isaacs," said Neil. "We might not have lasted another night on our own."

"This is going to be a very cold night," Isaacs looked at both of them as he spoke. "But you are safe now, we have plenty of food and lots of firewood at The Pigeon."

"Our feet have been frozen now for two week or more. They froze the first night we got ashore on November 26. I don't know what date it is now. We have lost track of time," said Neil.

"It is the twelfth day of December," Isaacs looked at a calendar on the wall.

"If that's the case, then we have been on the move for eighteen days," said Neil.

"We have not yet been introduced," said Isaacs. "I am Isaac Isaacs! I am the first English Newfoundlander and the caretaker for all the French rooms in this area. I have six men with me, we will do everything in our means for you."

"I'm Neil Dewar, this is Richard McFie, I was Purser on the *Rebecca*. We sailed under Captain Maxwell. Our friend is Charley Donaldson."

"When your friend gets here we will have supper. In the meantime, I am going to make you a mug of tea. It may settle your stomach."

"Thank you, sir, this is like coming into heaven," Neil spoke fervently and McFie nodded in agreement.

When Donaldson arrived he seemed worse than before. He could walk only if someone steaded him. He seemed to be in a state of shock when he first came in. When he was led into the house and placed on a wooden couch near the wall, he seemed to pass out. Isaacs went over to him and shook his shoulder. Half-conscious, Donaldson opened his eyes and looked around. He felt pain in every part of his body.

"How are you, son?" Isaacs asked.

"I'm dying, sir, please let me die."

Isaacs didn't comment as he hung a large iron pot filled with caribou stew over the fireplace. He said it would be ready in ten minutes.

"After we eat," he said to Neil, "we are going to get your boots off and bandage your feet. You will feel a lot better then."

Neil was anxious to get his boots off and have someone examine his feet. Isaacs went outside to have a look at the weather. When he returned, he informed everybody it was going to be a very cold night, and tomorrow would be stormy.

"The moon has the evening star let out on a long tow rope; it's a sign of a lot of wind," he said.

When the stew was warmed, the large pot was placed in the center of the table and everyone except Donaldson helped themselves as best as they could, using a large wooden ladle. Isaacs served Donaldson.

The stew was very thick, seventy percent meat, thirty percent vegetables and lots of gravy. After everyone had eaten their fill, Sam and Karl cleaned and stored away the dishes. Isaacs spread a punt sail on the wooden floor in front of the fireplace and told the three sailors that's where they would be sleeping.

After things got settled away, Isaacs told one of the Indians who had come over with Sam to go down to the shed and get a wooden tub and bring it to him. He said he also wanted two buckets of salt water.

The Indian he called John returned with a tub which was a beef barrel cut in half with holes cut in the sides for lifting it around. It looked and smelled clean. The other Indian he called George came in with two buckets of cold salt water right from the Atlantic ocean. He poured the water into the tub.

"Go down to the stage and bring up a gallon of coarse salt and throw it in the tub and mix it with the salt water," Isaacs ordered, and George did as he was told.

Isaacs brought out a large wooden box he called his medicine chest. He placed it on a stool near the table and opened the top. The house was silent. The only sound was the crackling of the fire and Isaacs moving around.

Reaching up on a shelf, he got a white earthenware pan, placed hot boiling water in it, and put it on the table. He went to another shelf and took down a leather case and brought it to the table. The case contained a scissors set that he put in the boiling water. He went to a trunk and got a couple of new knives and laid them in the hot water too. Then, he brought a lantern to the table, lit it, and turned it up as much as possible. All eyes were on him, wondering what he was going to do next.

"Neil, I am going to check you first," he said.

At a nod from Isaacs, Karl and George helped Neil to his feet and almost carried him over to a stool near the table. Neil wasn't the bravest of patients, but the pain in his feet and hands reminded him he had to get treatment or die.

"We'll have to remove your boots first, young man," Isaacs spoke in a stern voice. "I want to make it perfectly clear that I am not a medical doctor but I know more about medical treatment than most ordinary men. My ten years in the Royal Navy gave me a lot of experience."

Neil said he had spent twelve years in the Royal Navy, serving as a Lieutenant. Isaacs said they would have a long talk later.

Neil was sitting on the stool facing the tub of salt water. Isaacs said he needed a short block of wood for his patient to rest his feet on. Karl immediately went outside and brought in a block of wood about a foot long. The wood was placed near the tub of water and Neil's feet were gently placed upon it.

Isaacs rolled Neil's heavy pants and long underwear up above his knee. The underwear was inside his boot, dirty and full of dried blood. Neil was wearing laced up boots approximately three inches above the ankle. Isaacs used his scissors to cut the underwear off below the knee and down to the top of the boot; he could smell the stench of rotting flesh even before he touched the boot. He could also see a red streak going up the leg and there were signs of infection around the top of the boot. He had an idea what he would see when the boot came off. Isaacs tugged a little on the boot in the hope of removing it. It was stuck solid!

"I'm going to have to cut your boot down in order to remove it," he told Neil. He got a heavier pair of scissors out of his case and cut down both sides of the boot. He asked Karl to hold the lantern close to the foot to give him more light. "This may hurt a lot, Neil, but the boot has to come off so brace yourself."

Holding Neil's leg firmly, Isaacs worked hard to turn the top of the boot down around his heel. Even then, he had to pull on it several times to get it removed from the wool stocking which was stuck to it with blood and pus. Neil clamped his teeth and groaned in pain every time Isaacs touched his foot.

"I am going to put your foot in the tub of salty water and let it soak for a while. That will soften up the stocking before we remove it," said Isaacs.

Neil screamed as he put his foot in the cold briny water; it felt as though the salt cut to the bone. He clamped his teeth together, almost crushing them. In a few minutes the cold salty water relieved some of the burning in his foot, but not the pain.

"One boot off, one to go." Isaacs showed no mercy.

Neil told Isaacs about his knee, his right knee, and how he had damaged it while getting ashore. He knew the skin was ripped to the bone, and perhaps the knee was broken as well. Isaacs said he would look at it. But before he began working on the right foot, Isaacs went to his medical chest, found a short round piece of wood and put it on the table where he wound gauze around it two or three times. He showed it to Neil.

"When I tell you, put this between your teeth and bite on it whenever the pain gets hard. It will protect your teeth," he said.

Isaacs knew he would need help while examining the right leg so he asked Karl to assist him.

"Your job is to sit next to Neil," he told him. "Hold him and keep him steady and make sure he bites on the wooden pin if the pain gets too hard."

Isaacs rolled up the pants and underwear on Neil's right leg. What he saw was a frightening mess. The underwear was similar to a cast. It was hard with dried blood, but it wasn't attached to the knee. Isaacs cut the underwear above the knee and down to the boot. He then pulled it apart, revealing the awful infected cut on the knee.

"Put the pin between his teeth, this is going to hurt," he told Karl.

Isaacs felt the knee-bone as he pressed down on the cut. Neil screamed as his teeth sank into the wooden pin. The pain was too much for him to bear.

"You've got a bad gash on the knee." Isaacs looked up. "But it will heal and there are no bones broken."

Neil was gasping as though he would have a heart attack. The foot in the right boot was in exactly the same condition as the left one, full of dried blood and stuck to the stocking. Isaacs put the right foot down into the tub of brine water as Neil screamed.

"We have to keep you this way for at least ten minutes, then we will wash your foot in warm soapy water before attempting to remove the stocking." Isaacs dreaded to see what lay wrapped in the stockings; he knew it wasn't going to be pretty. Right now, the stench of rotting flesh filled the room and he could see that Neil's feet were beginning to swell, even in the cool water.

Isaacs looked at Neil's right hand, the back of it was infected and scabbed over. He could tell the skin was gone to the bone under the scabs. Neil also complained of a sore elbow.

After ten or fifteen minutes, Isaacs removed Neil's feet from the water, noticing that his feet and legs were purple with the cold. He then put Neil's feet into a wooden pan he filled with warm, soapy water.

"The stockings have to come off. Now, get a good grip on the wooden pin for this," he told Neil.

Isaacs got the scissors and started cutting the stocking down the heel and along the bottom of the foot. It was a gruesome task. Neil gripped the stool and clamped the wooden pin between his teeth as Karl held his left arm tightly. Isaacs peeled the stocking from one foot. Karl watched for a few seconds then turned away.

Isaacs knew that when the stockings came off it was going to cause bleeding. He'd already prepared a heavy bandage and had it close by on the table. As he removed the stocking, the flesh along the side of the foot came off with it, revealing a mass of corruption. All the flesh on the two smallest toes came off, as did the toenails. Neil's foot resembled that of a skeleton.

With Neil looking as though he would faint, Isaacs told Sam to get a cool wet cloth and place it on his forehead in the event he passed out. Blood was now oozing from Neil's foot. Isaacs took the large bandage he had prepared and put it over the foot. He secured it tightly, and then wrapped the foot in a heavy cloth.

"We have one foot done, one to go." Isaacs walked to the stove and got the kettle. "We will have a mug of tea, Neil, before we tackle the other foot."

Sam removed the wet cloth from Neil's forehead and placed it on the table. After watching Isaacs work on Neil's foot he thought he would have a mug of strong tea too; although he would much prefer a strong drink of rum.

After Isaacs finished his mug of tea he repeated the same procedure on the other foot. The condition of both feet was much the same.

"Karl," he said, "I want you to get one of the Indians and go down to the stage and open a barrel of cod oil and skim off a bucket of blubber. I'm going to make blubber poultices to use on the feet. It may help to heal them. At the very least, it will take away the burning."

It was after 8 p.m. when Isaacs finished up with Neil. By that time, the house was so filled with the stench of rotting feet mixed with the awful smell of cod liver oil blubber that it made it difficult to breath.

After Neil's feet and hands were bandaged, his dirty clothes were removed, and replaced with clean clothes, a little large but fine. He was then carried to a spot near the open fire and placed on a piece of schooner canvas with a punt's sail over him. He immediately went into a deep trance.

The next man to get treated was Donaldson, who by now was understandably very nervous and frightened. He was helped to the stool by Karl and John. Donaldson seemed dizzy and Karl had to help steady him after he sat down.

"Mr. Isaacs, I can't stop from shaking," said Donaldson. "It feels as though the chill has gone through my bones. Maybe it's the heat from the fireplace that's causing it."

Isaacs said his blood pressure must be up and assured him it would settle down in a few minutes. During the ordeal of removing Donaldson's boots, Isaacs found he was in even worse condition than Neil. Because his boots went nearly to his knees infection was further up his legs. He already had red streaks going to his groin. His two feet were rotting and it confounded Isaacs how the man could put his feet to the ground, let alone walk on them. The stench of his feet was unbearable. Isaacs gave him similar treatment to Neil. His hands were not as bad as Neil's and it did not take as long to do them.

McFie was the last to receive treatment. Except for the state of Neil's elbow and knees, there was very little difference in any of their conditions. Shortly before dawn, the three survivors were done. They had their wounds cleaned and plastered with fish blubber and Castile soap, and they were laid side by side under a punt's sail, fast asleep.

Chapter 17

THE PIGEON

It was December 12, 1816, when Isaac Isaacs removed the boots and stockings from the three sailors.

Early the next morning, Neil had an agonizing desire to relieve himself. He knew he couldn't walk so he attempted to crawl, but where would to go, he didn't know.

There was only one answer, to call Karl.

The fireplace was still burning so he knew someone was stoking it, someone was likely awake. In the dim light cast by the fire he called to Karl. A voice responded, inquiring of his needs, it was Isaacs.

"I need to get to the outhouse, sir," said Neil.

"Do you want to have a bowel movement or leak water?"

"Leak water."

"I put a hole in the floor for that purpose over by the wash stand. It's covered with a board, you'll see it."

Neil somehow managed to crawl across the floor as Isaacs asked him how he felt.

"I feel very good, sir," he answered. "The worst pain I have is in my elbow. My feet and knee feel fine."

"I'll work on your elbow after breakfast."

After Neil crawled back to his place and covered himself with the punt sail he heard Donaldson groaning.

Unless they were going on a trip somewhere or had something important to do, Isaacs asked his men to stay in their bunks until daybreak. He told them as well not to light the lanterns in the morning; he didn't want any oil burned when there wasn't need of it.

That did not keep George and John in the bunk, however. Every morning, they were up before daylight and hanging the iron kettle over the fire. This morning was no different.

Isaacs got up and went over to the three sailors. He asked Donaldson how he felt.

"I'm not very good, sir, got a lot of pain in my groin, I haven't slept all night," he replied.

"I have some wild roots I am going to steep out for you. You can have the drink after you get your breakfast. This is a drink that should take care of the pain."

Isaacs knew Donaldson was going to have a rough time recovering, if indeed he did recover. Both his legs were black to the knees; he had swollen glands around his groin and around the back of his neck, all sure signs of infection. Isaacs went outside and when he came back he told everyone a storm was brewing.

"We are going to have the wind southeast. A gale, big sea, and along with that we should have a big fall of snow." Isaacs told Sam to get lots of fire wood brought inside. "We'll need extra water brought in too; we are probably going to use a lot the next few days."

Breakfast was oatmeal flavoured with molasses and mixed with scraps of hard bread beat into small pieces. After breakfast was eaten and cleared away, Neil and McFie were brought to the table. Donaldson was unable to be moved; he had a high temperature and could barely open his eyes.

Isaacs was anxious to know something about the *Rebecca* and what she was doing around the Northern Peninsula of Newfoundland this late in the season. Neil told him the whole story, even about the affairs Captain Maxwell and the Mate were having with the women aboard.

"They weren't concerned about where the ship went or what kind of a storm was on; all they wanted was a good time below."

"The company that sent the ship to Cape Charles this time of the year must have been misinformed," Isaacs said. "By October, the wind blows from northwest to southeast most of the time. This is a dangerous time for the Cape Charles area."

"We spent a week trying to get into the harbour but never had the room to beat our way in because of the wind," said Neil.

"I know what you were up against. No ship should be near the Gulf of St. Lawrence this time of the year." Isaacs shook his head.

Neil told him about Emily Cummings, the girl he had met aboard and how he had promised to do everything possible to save her if the ship got into trouble.

"I'm not sure if I gave my all to save her, Mr. Isaacs. Maybe I could have done more. It haunts me every time I close my eyes."

"There's only so much a human being can do in those situations," Isaacs assured him.

Neil noticed that Isaacs kept referring to someone named Herb and wondering if they should go to The Pigeon before the storm came on.

Isaacs told him Herb stayed at the large bunkhouse in The Pigeon repairing fishing nets and baking all their bread. He usually had one Indian with him. Isaacs said he planned to move down to the larger house in The Pigeon in order to accomodate everyone. He said Sam would stay in his house with George.

"We can have two dog teams, four dogs to a team," said Karl. "That way, we only have to make two trips each. We should be able to do it fairly quickly."

"Yes, that's what we'll do," said Isaacs. "If we start now we should be moved there before the storm strikes."

"I can take you and two other men with me, as well as the things you want to carry down with you. I can make a round trip in about an hour," said Karl.

"Okay, get the two teams ready," said Isaacs.

Before Neil and McFie knew anything, they were on their way to The Pigeon.

It was not as easy to get Donaldson moved. He was very ill. Isaacs put a straw mattress on the sled for him to lie on. The young sailor had to be wrapped in heavy blankets and rolled up in a canvas tarpaulin before he was loaded on the sled. Sam had to go slowly and cautiously; even the small bumps in the trail caused him pain.

Chapter 18

DONALDSON AND McFIE

L'Anse au Pigeon was a summer fishing station located on the northeast side of Quirpon Island. It was inhabited by European fishermen during the days of John Cabot, the Italian born English explorer who discovered parts of North America in 1497, and is held to be the first European to travel to North America since the Norse Vikings in the eleventh century. Local folklore has it that John Cabot buried one of his shipmates there and marked his grave with a granite cross. Many years later, in 1700, the French of St Malo moved into the area and built their fishing premises in what they named L'Anse au Pigeon. They built large ovens nearby in which to bake bread, and also a slipway for small craft. The reason for building at The Pigeon was because it was closer to the fishing grounds and also had a good source of fresh drinking water. The reason Isaac Isaacs and his men became permanent residents of Newfoundland was to guard these fishing premises.

* * * * *

The storm Isaac Isaacs had predicted came on suddenly before noon. It came from the southeast with heavy snow and wind. By noon, it had developed into a major blizzard. By that time, Isaacs and his men, including the three sailors, were snug in what was called The House.

The House was equipped with a large cooking stove installed in the center of the building. It also had a fireplace to keep the extreme end of the building warm and comfortable. At one end of the building there were two rooms; one was usually occupied by Isaacs during the off season. This was when the French fishing captain had returned to France after the summer fishery was over. The House had a supply room on the side of the building where winter supplies of food and clothing were stored. The bunks in the rooms were made of boards which were fastened to the wall and covered with a straw mattress.

* * * * *

Donaldson arrived on the dog team driven by Sam. He was immediately carried to his bunk and placed on the straw mattress. He was groaning in pain and seemed on the brink of death.

Isaacs told Karl to take charge and get everything ready for the storm. He said they would need lots of water and firewood for the next few days. He whispered to Karl that Donaldson had lockjaw caused by infection and it was unlikely he would make it. Neil and McFie were placed in bunks close to the stove; they were still in bad shape, but tried not to show it. Neil was on the bunk for just a few minutes when he fell into a deep sleep.

After everyone was settled away, Isaacs told Herb to go to the stage to get a meal of seal meat.

"Take the big iron pot and fill it and we'll have enough for a couple of days. And while you're at it, bring back a couple of slabs of salt pork. I believe we've got everything else we need in the store-room," Isaacs looked out through the window and saw the storm coming on.

The southeast wind was beginning to push the swirling snow through the hills and valleys of Quirpon Island. Isaacs told Sam and the Indian to head back to the house at Grandmother's Cove before it got too stormy. He said to come back when the storm was over.

After Sam left, Isaacs attended to Donaldson, first asking how he felt. Donaldson said he felt very dizzy and as though the top of his head would come off at any minute.

Isaacs went to his medicine box and got a cloth. Then he went outside, got snow, rolled it in the cloth and placed it on Donaldson's forehead. In a few minutes he felt a little better. He told Donaldson he had herbs he was going to steep that might help as they were good to treat infection.

Donaldson tried not to whimper, he just groaned.

Isaacs decided to ignore the groans; he wanted to examine the sailor's feet and hands to get a better look at the condition they were in and to determine if the infection was spreading. He got a wooden basin, put warm water in it and mixed in a handful of rock salt.

Donaldson was nervous of Isaacs touching his feet.

"Mr. Isaacs," he said. "You will kill me if you touch my feet, they are burning as though they are on fire."

"I have got to attend to your feet. If I don't, they won't get better. Now, I am going to bathe them in warm water." Isaacs placed a sheet under Donaldson and removed the fish blubber poultice as the sailor cried out in pain. "I am going to wipe your leg with a warm damp cloth, it may hurt a little."

Isaacs told Karl to assist him. What they were looking at was unbelieveable. Donaldson's leg was swollen to twice its normal size and it was black above the knee. The whole front of his leg was a bag of pus, even around the knee cap.

"I am going to have to scrape away the pus to control the spread of infection to the upper leg. The pus is what's giving you the pain," said Isaacs.

Donaldson didn't seem to be paying attention; he simply stared at the ceiling. Isaacs knew he would have trouble working on Donaldson's legs where he was. He had to get him somewhere where someone could hold him down. There was no doubt he would be screaming and out of control when he began his treatment.

He rejected the idea of using the kitchen table. On one side of the large kitchen there was a six foot long chart table, used in winter as a catch-all. Isaacs thought the table would be a good place to perform the procedure. He told Donaldson they were going to put him on the chart table and clean his legs, and assured him everything would be fine.

The chart table was pulled into the center of the room and Isaacs covered it with a grey boat's sail. By now it was getting very tense in the kitchen. The smell of cooking seal meat combined with the odour from the fish blubber poultices and the stench of rotting flesh made the air foul and almost impossible to breathe. None of it bothered Isaac Isaacs. He was busy getting everything ready in order to scrap Donaldson's legs.

The sailor was brought to the chart table and laid on it. Donaldson had lost a lot of weight. His eyes were sunken and dark and he yelled in agony every time he was moved. Isaacs instructed Herb and Karl to stand on each side of the patient and hold his arms.

"Hold him down if he starts acting up," he told them.

Herb called Isaacs to one side and whispered to him.

"I think it would be much better, Skipper, if we tied him down to the table," he said.

Isaacs agreed.

Herb went out to the store-room and brought back several pieces of rope which they used to tie Donaldson to the table. It was not what Isaacs wanted but it had to be done in order to try to save the sailor's life.

Herb wore a pair of wool mittens soaked in warm water in order to handle the leg Isaacs was to work on. Isaacs gave

Donaldson the block of wood and said to bite on it when he started scraping his legs. Donaldson said he would!

Isaacs started on the right leg, using the back of a pair of scissors to scrape away the pus. It's likely L'Anse au Pigeon has never since heard such screams as Charley Donaldson emitted on that fateful day.

As Herb and Karl tried to hold him, their hearts were torn. They had never experienced anything like it before. Herb began sobbing.

Every time Isaacs pulled the back of the scissors down the skinless, infected, blackened legs, Charley screamed in pain.

He called to his mother, and he cursed Captain Maxwell and everyone else associated with the shipwreck that had caused his problems.

Before Isaacs was finished Charley Donaldson had gone into a coma. Except for his breathing, one would assume he was dead.

"I should remove his legs at the knees while he is unconscious," said Isaacs."They are going to have to come off to save his life... On the other hand, I had better wait and see the results of this experiment."

When the scraping was finished, Isaacs rubbed the bleeding legs with cod liver oil and wrapped them in cloth. They removed the ropes used to tie Donaldson to the table and put him back into his bunk.

Neil and McFie were sleeping when the ordeal began, but they were awakened by Donaldson's screams and subsequently witnessed what Neil referred to as the butchering of Charley.

* * * * *

After the Donaldson treatment, Isaacs asked John and the Indian called Matthew if the seal meat was ready for dinner.

"Have you attended to the bake pot?" he asked John.

"Pot lots of water, ready," he said.

"I am going to make a pastry to go on the pot, get me some flour and water," Isaacs washed his hands, made a large pastry with the flour and water and placed it on the seal meat. He then put the pot back over the fire to cook.

The seal meat with pastry on top was delicious. Herb served Neil and McFie in their bunks. Donaldson did not move, just groaned in his sleep. After dinner was cleared away, Isaacs went outside to check on the weather. When he returned, he gave everyone an update.

"A huge sea is beginning to heave from the southeast accompanied by a lot of snow. I would say we will have snow drifts five or six feet high before this is over," he said.

"It's all right if the sea doesn't come in over the meadow. I suppose the boats are all right," said Herb. He looked after the fishing gear in The Pigeon.

"I don't think it will be as bad as you think, but then again you never know," said Karl.

"We should go down and run a few lines from the boats to one of the ring bolts. At least they won't go out with the sea," said Herb.

"Yes, you should," said Isaacs. After Karl and Herb had dressed and gone outside, Isaacs went to McFie and told him he was going to have a look at his injuries.

"How do you feel, Richard?" he asked.

"My two feet and legs are burning as if a flame were on them," he told Isaacs.

"I am going to have a look at them in a few minutes."

McFie shuddered. He didn't want to go through what Donaldson had just undergone. He would rather die first!

"Donaldson is a very sick man, I think he has lockjaw and I don't have anything to treat it. If he has it and we can't treat it you know what will happen, I don't have to tell you, the same goes for you." Isaacs looked sombre.

McFie lay still and closed his eyes, wondering if he would ever see his home again or had his time come.

As the blizzard raged outside, the clock on the side board rang 1 p.m. A few minutes later, Herb and Karl appeared, brushing snow off their clothes.

"It's a terrible day, the winds are about eighty miles per hour, We are darned lucky to have a roof over our heads. It certainly wouldn't be a good day on the ocean," said Karl.

"It's not a good day anywhere today," said Isaacs. "After Karl and Herb get their clothes hung up, we will have a look at your feet and legs and see what we have to do with them." Although McFie had his eyes closed he knew Isaacs was talking to him. "Yes sir," he said.

"If the infection has gone above your knees and there are red streaks up to your groin," Isaacs continued, "I will have to scrap your legs to try and get rid of the infection before it spreads to the rest of your body. You will have no choice but to lose both of your legs at your knees. It's your only hope of survival."

It was not what McFie wanted to hear. He knew things didn't look good, but to lose his legs to his knees by a butcher who did not fully understand what he was doing, well, that was unthinkable! McFie asked Neil what he thought of the idea of losing his legs to save his life.

"I suppose we have no other choice if it comes to that," said Neil. "We can wait and see what happens to Donaldson, see if he survives without losing his legs."

"I can't bear the thought of my legs being scraped with the back of a pair of cobbler's scissors. I think I'll go out of my mind with pain," McFie said.

"Just grip your teeth and bear it, Richard. My turn is coming; I'm going to have to do it too," said Neil.

Herb and Karl were ready to assist Isaacs in treating McFie. The three men placed McFie on the chart table.

Isaacs sterilized his scissors in boiling water. Herb again put the ropes around the table and tied McFie down. He placed the wooden pin in his mouth and instructed him to bite down on it should the pain became too much for him to bear.

"I am going to clean all the infection away from your legs. I may be able to wash it away first. If I can't, I will have to scrape it away. It's going to be painful, but just do as you are told," he said. When Isaacs gently touched McFie's legs he started screaming, tenderness was everywhere. It was going to be a heartbreaking job.

The fish blubber poultices were stuck to the flesh in several places. As Isaacs removed them he tore the flesh which caused bleeding. McFie's two legs, from four inches below the knees to the top of his toes, were infected. The skin on his toes was completely gone. Isaacs realized he would have to remove his legs at the knees if he was to save his life. But... he wouldn't do it yet. He wanted to try and see if there was some way he could control the bleeding.

Isaacs removed the pus and corruption as best he could from McFie's legs and feet. He knew his hands were as bad as his feet, but they could wait. McFie's screams were as bad as Donaldson's.

Isaacs came to the same conclusion as he had with Donaldson. He would have to amputate McFie's two legs at the knees if he were to save his life. However, he would deal with that tomorrow.

* * * * *

As the fifteenth of December rolled around, a huge sea rolled into L'Anse au Pigeon, bringing slob ice that piled up on the rocky shoreline. Herb and Karl left before daybreak to see if the boats had moved; they returned and reported all was well, but a big sea was rolling over the bond (the grassy area back from the high water mark where cod traps and nets were spread out and repaired during the fishing season).

* * * * *

All day, those in The House watched Donaldson wrestling with death. It was plain to see he wouldn't last another day. During the night the young sailor woke and called Neil to come near. He said he wanted to tell him something. Neil couldn't walk, so Isaacs had Herb and Karl carry him to Donaldson.

"I am dying, Neil," he said. "I want you to tell my mother I love her and will meet her again in heaven some day." He told Neil how to contact his mother and went on to say, "I would not be in this condition if Captain Maxwell had listened to you. Now we will all probably die because of his stupid acts. Tell our story to the newspapers back home."

During the rest of the night Donaldson screamed in his sleep; it appeared he was quarrelling with someone, trying to get them to listen. A little after dawn, the sailor started biting his hands and screaming. There was nothing Isaacs or anyone else could do.

Donaldson was at the point of death. At 11 a.m. he was again seized with an uncontrollable state of mental delirium and died. He was thirty years old.

There now were only two survivors left.

* * * * *

Isaacs knew there would be a problem digging a grave for Donaldson. The ground was frozen like steel; the shovels they had to use were made of wood.

"It will be nearly impossible to bury him in the ground at this time of the year," he told Karl.

"If we had a boat launched, we could bury him at sea," said Karl.

"We won't be able to launch a boat after this storm; the shoreline will be iced up. We'll have to put him in the loft at the stage and wait for a better time," said Isaacs.

Donaldson's body was rolled in canvas, carried to the store loft, and secured from the dogs. He would be buried in the spring, or maybe sent to a watery grave at sea after the ice left. For more than a week after Donaldson's death, Isaacs tried everything he knew to treat the remaining two survivors for infection and high fever. There was, however, no improvement in their condition. If anything, they seemed to get worse, especially McFie.

It was getting close to Christmas.

Isaacs did not want to have Neil and McFie lying in bed on Christmas Day with their arms and legs gone. However, he did not want them lying in bed dying with no hope on Christmas morning either. He wondered what to do. On Christmas Eve, he concluded that the only way for them to survive was to remove their limbs.

"Both of you will die of blood poisoning if your feet and hands are not removed," he told them. "Your feet are the worst. Your toes have rotted off, it's impossible for your feet to get better. They wouldn't heal even if you were in a hospital. The doctors would remove them immediately."

The two men agreed, they were only too well aware of their sad condition. "I am going to see if I can stop the infection," said Isaacs. "But in two days if there's no improvement I will have to remove your limbs. That will be done right after Christmas Day."

It was not very encouraging news for the two sailors who were listening intently as doom seemed to stare them in the face. There was no doubt McFie was in much worse condition than

Neil. The sooner he had his ordeal over, the better chance he had of surviving.

Isaacs looked at Neil's knee and elbow and noticed a slight improvement. They had not frozen, but Neil had torn the flesh to the bone on the rocks. Isaacs said his knee and elbow stood a chance of getting better, but his feet had to come off. It wasn't pleasant news for Neil.

* * * * *

It was Christmas Eve. Isaacs' men were busy all day, feeding and watering the dogs, keeping the wood and water topped up, and keeping an eye on the boats.

Neil and McFie talked about what Isaacs had said about them losing their limbs. They realized this would be a major operation. There were a lot of questions they wanted to ask. But, then, would it matter? Nothing they asked was going to change anything.

During the afternoon, Herb made a batch of pancakes and fried them in seal oil. They were eaten with molasses spread on them.

McFie was not well enough to eat. During the afternoon, he started complaining about pains in his head and groin. He was also flushed and burning with fever. McFie was in a lot of pain. He knew infection was spreading through his body, he could feel glands swelling in his groin and on the back of his neck. He knew he could not wait another two days. It might be too late.

McFie called Isaacs to his bunk and asked him if he knew the symptoms of blood poisoning and lockjaw. Isaacs said he did. McFie showed him the swollen glands in his groin and said he had them under both of his arms and around the back of his neck as well.

"I know. You were like that yesterday too," said Isaacs. "There's no doubt about it, Richard, blood poisoning has set in. I will give you till tomorrow morning. If everything is still the same, you know what has to be done."

McFie knew what had to be done, he would have to lose both his legs and arms. Despondent, he turned into the wall and sobbed.

* * * * *

Isaacs knew time was running out for McFie. If he was going to remove his legs he would have to do it right away. Twenty-four hours could be too long to wait; infection was spreading rapidly. Isaacs had never performed an amputation on an animal or a person and the very thought of cutting off a man's legs was not something he was looking forward to. Herb and Karl came to his room for a discussion. If they were going to be his helpers, he wanted to know what they thought of it. First, he told them he would operate on McFie in his room behind a closed door. He did not want Neil to hear or see what was going on as he could lose his nerve when his time came!

Isaacs explained what had to be done. Herb wouldn't agree to help at first; he wanted no part of watching a man's legs being cut off. He was aghast that Isaacs was going to do it, saying that type of surgery was only performed by doctors in hospitals. He said even on the battlefield it was doctors who performed amputations.

"If I don't do it, who will?" asked Isaacs.

"Leave them alone, count me out, let them die a peaceful death if they must. Removing their legs may kill them anyway," said Herb.

"If we leave them as they are they won't die a peaceful death. You saw the way Donaldson died. Do you want to see these men die the same way when we might be able to save their lives by removing their legs?" asked Isaacs.

For a long minute, there was silence.

"I can see it your way, Mr. Isaacs," said Karl finally.

"It's not the fact you don't know what you're doing, sir. The fact is I don't want to take part in it." said Herb, knowing all the while he would be forced to help.

Isaacs was not happy with Herb. "Okay Herb," he said. "I'm not going to force you to take part in the affair. I understand. Karl and I will have to try to do it by ourselves."

Herb rubbed his hands together; he knew the importance of saving lives, he had seen most everything in his lifetime. Although he still couldn't come to grips with the thought of cutting off a man's legs on Christmas Eve, what other choice was there?

"Okay, Mr. Isaacs, I'll do my best," he said. "If I faint you'd better have a cold cloth ready to put on my forehead and bring me back, I don't want to join Donaldson up in the store loft."

"Thanks, Herb. You know, you may not even see me cutting off the legs. What I want you to do is make sure the wooden block is in McFie's mouth at all times and that he's biting on it. Talk to him, try to keep him distracted. What we are going to do is bring the chart table into the bedroom and let him stay in here for a few days to recover."

"How do you intend to remove the legs? Will you be cutting both of them off together, or have a rest period between each one?" asked Karl.

"As soon as we get the first one off and bandaged, we'll take the other one off. The quicker we get it done the better," said Isaacs.

"Have you ever done anything like this in your life?" Herb asked Isaacs.

"No, never. I've heard where people had to remove toes and fingers but never legs and arms," said Isaacs.

"Maybe McFie would rather Neil have his legs off first. We should ask," said Karl.

"McFie is in a much worse condition than Neil, we don't have any time to lose; we have to stop the spread of infection as soon as we can," said Isaacs.

"Okay," said Karl, "Let's get at it."

* * * * *

Isaacs knew what he had to do. To start, he would need lots of bandages and strings. Fishing line could be used as tourniquets to stop the bleeding. And he would have to tear up old shirts left by the French fishermen for bandages. Also, he would need a chisel, hammer and extra knives. These items would have to be very sharp and sterilized in hot water. He sent Herb to the work shed to get the small bench axe and a couple of chisels, as well as some fishing line and one of the new wooden mallets they had made last week.

Herb and Karl headed for the store-room on the wharf while Isaacs started making bandages. Neil and McFie were talking, their bunks were not far apart.

"What do you think our chances would be if we refused to let Isaacs take off our legs?" McFie sounded frantic. "I don't think he's ever done anything like this before. How will he control the bleeding? Where will he get the stitching material? I think I have a right to know all that."

"I don't know, but I am certain he has something in mind or he would not attempt to do it." Neil tried to sound calm and confident.

"If I die from the operation and you live, I want you to tell my relatives what happened. Why we found ourselves into this situation in the first place. Make sure you tell it all if you survive." McFie was looking at him wildly.

Neil looked into his eyes and promised he would. "You do the same for me," he said. "Tell my father and mother what happened to me on this Christmas Eve. Tell them everything."

McFie started crying, he was in terrible pain and burning with a fever. His thoughts were back home in England. His mother was probably getting a goose ready to cook for a feast on Christmas Day.

And here he was having to decide if he should have his two legs cut off by a man who knew nothing more than cutting heads off cod fish. But what else could he do? He knew he would die soon if he didn't have it done.

McFie wept bitterly! When he regained his composure he said that maybe Neil should have the operation first.

"If that's what Mr. Isaacs wants, I'll go first," said Neil.

The two men could hear the rustle and bustle of Isaacs and his assistants getting ready. To them, it sounded like a butcher making preparations in a butcher shop.

When Isaacs came out of the bedroom he asked them how they were feeling and wished them Merry Christmas.

"Richard, is there anything you want to tell Neil before we take you into the other room?" he asked McFie.

Neil spoke up, "Mr. Isaacs, sir, we have decided that I will have my legs off first. Richard is nervous about going first. He would rather it be me."

Isaacs said nothing for a minute and then he spoke directly to Neil.

"If I leave Richard until tomorrow I have a feeling it will be too late. He is in worse condition than you. And the thing is, I can only do one of you today. It will be getting dark in a couple of hours and the operation has to be done in daylight. I can't do it by torch light."

McFie knew Isaacs was right and even though he was hesitant, he agreed.

McFie put his arms around Neil and wept. The pain in his hands was too severe for hugs or handshakes. He assured Neil he was the best friend he ever had, and said he hoped to see him in the morning.

Neil wished him all the best.

Richard McFie was taken to the inside room at 2 p.m. He was very frightened and shaking uncontrollably. Isaacs asked him if he was cold, and he replied in a trembling voice that he wasn't.

After the bedroom door was closed and McFie was put on the chart table, which had been put by the window, Karl put a loop of rope around one of his arms arm close to the elbow. Herb did the same with his other arm. Another rope was secured across his chest with heavy cloth underneath. After his pants were removed both his legs were spread apart and securely tied above the knees.

"Oh my God, oh my God what will happen to me?" cried McFie.

He knew he would have a hard time, but it was too late to change his mind. He had agreed to the operation and knew he had to have it. All his crying and pleading would not change the mind of Isaac Isaacs. His legs were coming off and that was that!

Isaacs spread a blanket over McFie, covering him from above his knees to his chin. He told Herb to put a cold cloth on his forehead and get ready to put the block of wood in the sailor's mouth.

Isaacs had the cutting instruments in hot water and he'd washed his hands as clean as possible. He instructed Karl to cut off two feet of fishing line. He would use it as a tourniquet above the knee before he commenced cutting.

Isaacs put fishing line around McFie's leg and pulled it tight, using the handle of a knife. With this done he stopped the flow of blood to the leg.

Karl could not believe what he was about to witness. He'd heard many tales about people losing limbs. He had seen men cut themselves badly while working in the fishing industry. But he'd never seen anything like what was happening before his eyes right now. Here was a man using a chisel, a wooden mallet, a carpenter's axe and fish knives, and he had a cobbler's needle stuck in the wall waiting to sew raw edges of skin together.

Isaacs did a very poor job removing the first leg; blood spattered everywhere over the table.

It was difficult holding McFie still enough to make the proper incisions and the result was that the cuts were jagged and uneven. At one point, when Isaacs put the chisel between the leg bone and the thigh bone to gave it a knock to separate it, McFie screamed loudly. That made Karl jump.

Isaacs roared, "For God's sake, Herb, keep the block of wood in his mouth."

"Yes, sir, I'm doing my best," Herb seemed ready to bolt through the door.

As Isaacs worked on the amputation, Herb thought McFie had stopped breathing. But suddenly he gave a loud scream and sent the wooden block skittering across the floor. Herb retrieved it and put it back in his mouth.

The operation took longer than anyone had anticipated and had to be finished by lamp light.

The greatest problem was controlling the bleeding. It was impossible to leave the tourniquets wound tight above the knees, but as soon as they were slackened, blood flowed freely from the wound.

After his legs were removed, McFie lay in a state of delirium. He looked as though he was dead. His vital signs were irregular and his entire body was shaking. Isaacs and Karl knew his chances of survival were slim. Isaacs told Karl and Herb not to disturb him for a few hours.

"Leave him as he is and we will see what happens," Isaacs put large pieces of cloth over the leg stumps and compressed them. But even then, he was unable to stop the bleeding.

After a great pouring out of blood, McFie died in the early hours of Christmas morning.

Before the sun came up, Karl and Herb had rolled the body of Richard McFie into a canvas bag, putting his severed legs by his side. With sober dignity, they put his body on a hand barrow and carried it to the store-room loft. There he joined his friend, Donaldson, while they both waited for their final voyage out of L'Anse au Pigeon.

Chapter 19

CHRISTMAS DAY

Neil knew something terrible had happened to McFie. He'd heard the rushing about during the night, and the whispering between the men. He didn't ask but he suspected that Richard had met the same fate as Donaldson.

Matthew came over to Neil. Matthew held his nose and screwed up his face as he pointed to the pot of salt fish he had cooking in the fireplace. The smell of salt fish filled the kitchen, but it also had the effect of concealing the stench of blubber and rotting flesh that permeated the house.

Neil lay quietly in his bunk, although his feet and hands were burning. He was waiting for Mr. Isaacs to tell him the sad news about McFie and to advise him when his turn would come to have his legs removed.

The only light in the long kitchen came from the fireplace where flickering flames made long shadows on the wooden walls. Neil heard Herb saying something about it being time to get the brewis ready and the pork fried out. The men were making fisherman's brewis, cod fish cooked with hard tack and pork fat. Karl said Herb would have to do it all himself as he knew the most about cooking.

Shortly after daylight, Isaacs came and talked to Neil.

"On this Christmas morning I have bad news to break. I should be wishing you a Happy Christmas but I can't. Richard passed away last night after the operation. It was impossible to stop the flow of blood. It may have been due to the massive infection in his bloodstream. But his blood would not clot and he consequently bled to death. We did our very best to save him." Isaacs was despondent. He wiped tears from his eyes.

Isaacs then examined the backs of Neil's hands and what was left of his fingers. The only way he could describe it was mass corruption. There was hardly any flesh left on Neil's fingers. His hands were black and swollen and infected all the way to his wrists. Isaacs did not comment as he examined Neil's hands, but he was certain they would have to come off.

Then he looked at his feet. There was little difference in the condition of either foot. He was certain they would have to come off as well if he were to save his life. Neil didn't seem to have too high a temperature which was a good sign. Isaacs said nothing as he walked away from Neil. He rubbed his hands as he went to the bedroom where he had operated on McFie. On his way, he motioned for Karl to follow him.

After the door was shut, the two men sat on a bench near the wall and stared sadly at the chart table. Their thoughts were with McFie.

"I had a close look at Neil's hands and feet," Isaacs told Karl. "They are decaying more and more every hour because of infection. There is no choice but to amputate immediately. The infection must be stopped to save his life."

"Do you think his chances are any better than McFie's?"

"No," Isaacs answered. "Unless we do it differently and find a way to tie the main arteries to control the bleeding. If we can't do that there's not much point in operating because the same thing will happen to him."

"We have to do something different, sir."

Isaacs stared at the ceiling.

Karl said, "When you began to remove McFie's first leg, I heard Herb say you were doing it wrong. He mumbled something about you were doing it wrong and McFie would bleed to death."

Isaacs looked at Karl with eyes blazing, "What in the name of God do you mean?"

"I don't know what Herb meant, but that's what he said." Karl was nervous.

"Why didn't you tell me this before. Maybe Herb knows something we don't," said Isaacs.

"I don't know, you should ask him, sir."

"Yes, we'll ask him now. Tell him to come in I want him."

Karl summoned Herb who came into the room and shut the door. Isaacs gave him quite a stare.

"Karl just told me what you said when I started to remove McFie's legs. You said I did it the wrong way. What did you mean by that?" he asked.

For a moment Herb did not know what to say. He didn't want to have a dispute with Mr. Isaacs. But at last he spoke up, he knew he had to.

"When you started to remove the first leg, I thought you were doing it wrong by cutting it off at the joint. That's all I meant, sir," Herb looked at Isaacs.

"Explain to us how you would have done it differently to make the operation a success," Isaacs was very curious.

Herb felt bad, he did not want to be drawn into this. But if he was put on the spot he must explain himself.

"Well sir, this is what I would have done, if I had been you," he said. "You know what is done when we chop off a dog's tail. We tie a firm line around the tail above where we are going to make the chop. This stops the blood by sealing off the main artery. Then we tighten it again below the bone after it retracts up the tail. Following that, we burn the severed place with a red hot iron and that causes a crust to form. After a day or two we take the line off and the blood is stopped."

"Good god, Herb, you should have told me all of that before. It makes perfect sense."

"I didn't want to interfere, sir. You were doing the job."

Isaacs was silent. Perhaps he had erred. Perhaps he had not put enough thought into what he did with McFie.

Herb said, "I think you have a hacksaw here, Mr. Isaacs. All we have to do is sterilize the blade to saw the bones and heat a strip of iron to burn the area where we cut. I know where there is a piece of iron two inches wide, a quarter inch thick and a foot or so long."

"Okay, Herb, get the iron, put it in the fire, and bring me the hacksaw so that I can sterilize it."

Isaacs stood up as Herb and Karl left the house and went to the store-room.

Chapter 20
NEIL'S AGONY

There were no greetings or carol singing on this Christmas Day in L'Anse au Pigeon.

Neil was quiet, he was as white as a ghost and shaking. He felt like a criminal on death row, waiting for the executioner to lead him to the gallows.

For a moment he felt no pain in his hands at all. He attempted to pull his hair. But his hands fell at his side and he realized he had no fingers. He wondered what he should do. Should he run out into the storm and plunge into the briny, freezing Atlantic and end it all quickly? But how could he do that when he couldn't walk? He couldn't even stand on his decaying feet.

"I am a prisoner," he thought as he turned to the wall and wept. "The only choice I have is to wait for the executioner and be content with my trip into eternity."

Karl usually fed Neil his meals. On this Christmas morning he brought him strong black tea with brown sugar and boiled salt fish. There was as well soft brown bread with molasses, a Christmas treat.

Karl wondered how Neil felt about the upcoming operation. He could see the tears in his eyes and the grief on his face and knew he was terrified.

But Neil said he felt pretty good, even though he knew he was going to lose both his feet and probably his hands. He said they were no good to him as they were. His fingers and toes were rotting off.

"Don't be too disheartened about it, Neil," said Karl. "I think you are going to beat the odds. Mr. Isaacs is planning to operate on you differently than he did on Richard. He says you will be fine."

Neil felt a glimmer of hope. Maybe he would survive after all.

After breakfast, they all said a prayer for Neil. Isaacs knew he was going to have a very hard morning. The sound of hard leather boots on a wooden plank floor broke the silence as Karl and Herb came to get him. No matter how much he screamed, kicked, or yelled, his two legs and arms were coming off. Neil was carried into the bedroom and placed on the chart table.

A basin of boiling water with tools in it sat on a stool nearby. The pieces of rope used to tie McFie hung down loosely like branches from a limp plant.

The hacksaw blade had been scrubbed clean, boiled in hot water to sterilize it, and tightened firmly into the wooden frame. Isaacs opened the window a couple of inches, not only to let in fresh air, but to break the tension and to reduce the odour of rotting flesh.

Each man had a job. Herb stood by with a damp cool cloth to put on Neil's forehead and the block of wood for him to bite into when the pain became too severe. Karl's task was to help apply the tourniquets and hold the leg while Isaacs cut it with the hacksaw. Isaacs told them before they began, the plan was that if the patient passed out, Herb was not to apply a cool cloth to his forehead.

"If Neil passes out while I'm at the leg don't try to revive him until it's over. That way he might not feel as much pain," said Isaacs.

Matthew and John left the house shortly before the operation began and went to the work shed. At around nine thirty, Isaacs washed Neil's legs with soapy water and surveyed the area where he would cut first. That was halfway between the ankle and the knee.

"After I cut the leg, you will have to hold the foot as firmly as possible," he said to Karl. "Then, I will pull the skin back toward the knee as far as I can and hold it there while I saw off the two bones. When the leg is off, you will have to help me put a string above the area where we removed the leg. The bone should be up into the leg two or three inches, when this is tightened it should close off all the blood vessels. After we get the string on and tightened, you bring me the hot iron to put a crust on the wound."

Karl cringed but said nothing.

"Okay, we're all set to go," said Isaacs.

Using the back of a knife as leverage, he and Karl tightened the tourniquet as tight as possible around Neil's leg above the knee, shutting off the flow of blood below it.

"Open your mouth now, Neil, and bite on the wood." Herb said as he glanced at Isaacs. Neil did as he was told.

Isaacs lifted the leg as Karl placed a round block of wood underneath it, close to where it would be amputated. Isaacs chose one of the fish knives from the basin of hot water, then turned to Neil and made a deep incision across the back of the leg, cutting the skin to the bone. He also made a cut on each side to the bone.

Herb heard a loud groan and saw the muscles in Neil's face tighten as his teeth sank into the wood. His body heaved and nearly lifted from the table. Neil was wide-eyed. Herb placed the damp cool cloth on his forehead, hoping it would give him some relief.

It took only a few seconds for the blood in Neil's leg, from the cut down, to run out. With this done, Isaacs cut the skin across the front and around the shin bone. After all the flesh was cut, he pushed it back toward the knee approximately three inches, revealing the two leg bones.

"Give me the hacksaw, Karl," he held out his hand.

Karl quickly handed him the saw and went back to holding Neil's feet. Isaacs put the teeth on the bone close to his fingers and started sawing. As the saw dug into his shin bone, Neil let out a piecing scream that Herb never forgot. Telling the story many years later, Herb said although it happened long ago he could still hear the sound of Neil Dewar screaming as he went to sleep.

It took less than a minute for the hungry teeth of the hacksaw to dig into the large shin bone; the smaller leg bone was likewise quickly severed. Karl stood with Neil's lower leg in his hands. For a moment it seemed he would drop it as he slowly turned and put it gently on the floor.

"Give me the line to tie around the stump," said Isaacs. Karl got the line and held the leg stump for Isaacs to put a loop around it as a tourniquet and he pulled it tight.

"Hold to this end, Karl, as we tighten the line to tie it," said Isaacs. Karl held the end and they tightened the line.

"Get the hot iron," ordered Isaacs and Karl dashed to the fireplace where he wrapped a piece of cloth around the hot piece of iron and brought it to Isaacs on a plate.

"Now hold the leg tight, Karl, this could be painful," Isaacs took the hot iron and pressed it on the raw flesh of the leg stump.

Karl heard the hissing sound as the hot iron came in contact with the flesh. Neil gave a loud scream that echoed throughout the building.

"My God, you're killing me," he managed to say before Herb put the wooden plug in his mouth. It did very little to silence him because Neil passed out.

Three times, Isaacs repeated the procedure, burning the leg stump to a crust.

"That should do it, it's sealed. We'll get some turpentine to complete the job," Isaacs wiped the sweat from his brow.

(Turpentine is a very sticky substance, the resin of a conifer, especially fir, which is used in home remedies.)

Herb placed a cold wet cloth on Neil's forehead and shook him, calling his name at the same time. Neil opened his eyes and groaned. He called out a name Herb didn't know but the important thing was that he was conscious.

"One leg off and one to go, we'll remove the tourniquet above the knee within an hour to see if there is any bleeding," said Isaacs.

Karl was sure there would be no bleeding because the tourniquet near the end of the stump and the hot iron had sealed the wound. As they prepared the tools to remove the other leg, Isaacs turned to Neil and asked him how he felt. Neil kept his eyes closed and groaned as though he was dying.

"We removed the right leg successfully," Isaacs said. "There is no bleeding and all is well. We will begin the other leg soon."

Herb seemed ill. He knew he would never be able to go through the ordeal of helping to remove Neil's other leg. Trying to hold him down during the operation and listening to him screaming took the good out of him and made him feel so weak he thought he would faint.

Karl saw Herb's nerves were failing him and he suggested he go outside and get some fresh air. Herb told Karl he couldn't help with Neil anymore. Karl said he couldn't give up now. He said without his help Isaacs wouldn't be able to carry out the operation to save Neil's life.

"I know it's tough!" Karl patted Herb's back. "We're both the same, but we've got to help the skipper do what he has to do. Hang on, Herb, it won't take long."

Herb didn't want Karl's advice. He attempted to run to the shed and hide, but Karl stopped him.

"You can't run away, we need you!" Karl grabbed him by the shirt collar and dragged him back into the house.

Isaacs had an idea what was going on when he saw Karl holding Herb's collar. It made him mad, and he told Herb to smarten up and be civilized or they would be doomed.

"Be civilized, Skipper?" Herb was aghast. "Sawing the legs and arms off humans is civilized? What do you think I am anyway?"

"We have to save Neil Dewar's life at any cost with or without you. Without you, however, we might not be able to do it successfully. We need your help, Herb, so smarten up," Isaacs spoke sternly.

Herb knew Isaacs was right, but he still didn't see how he could continue helping with the amputations. It was like working in a slaughter house. He had seen two men slaughtered already; he didn't want to see the third one.

"Have a cup of tea, Herb, it will help calm your nerves," Karl spoke quietly and calmly.

"No tea," Isaacs sounded gruff. "We don't have time for tea. We've got a job to do. Let the three of us get at it and get it over with."

Herb hesitated for a moment then he went back to the room where Neil lay strapped to the chart table. Neil had heard every word and was now staring at the ceiling.

"One leg is off, I guess I'll lose the other one soon?"

Neil kept his eyes on the ceiling as he spoke. Herb wiped his face and said nothing.

"What will they do with my leg now it has been cut off?" Neil asked.

Herb couldn't answer him, he was in no position to discuss the missing leg. He couldn't understand how Neil could talk about it.

Isaacs had the tools ready to remove the second leg, and he now had a better idea of how to do it. He told Karl he should be able to remove the leg in about fifteen minutes after the tourniquet was in place. He went on to try and rally Herb.

"Listen to me, Herb," he said. "You have a job to do and you have to do it the same as you did before. You don't have to look at us. The important thing is... don't leave Neil's side... this is not going to take very long."

Herb agreed to do his best, to stay and see it through.

Removing Neil's second leg went better than the first one, although the yells, screams and pleas for help were even more intense and forever unforgettable.

Herb held Neil's head and wept with him as Isaacs sawed off the leg bones. As the saw started to enter the tibia bone, Neil started shaking and his whole body began to tremble. For an awful moment, Herb thought his heart had stopped.

"I think he is dead, sir," Herb's voice quivered.

Isaacs glanced at Neil while continuing his work. He had no time to examine the patient. He was removing the leg, and whether Neil was dead or alive it was coming off.

Herb removed the cold wet cloth that covered the upper part of Neil face and looked at his eyes. Only the whites showed. Herb took the wooden block from between Neil's teeth and was about to pronounce him dead. He jumped as Neil suddenly screamed and shouted that they were murdering him.

"It will be over soon, the job will be completed. Not much longer, Neil," Isaacs spoke gently.

Neil made an unusual movement and almost came off the table. The bone that was half sawed snapped, leaving a pointed edge that Isaacs didn't see as he proceeded on with the operation. The leg came off in Karl's hands, he turned around and put it on the floor as before.

"Get the line and help me put it around the stump," Isaacs said to Karl. We have lots of room to tie it... the bones have gone further up into the leg."

A few minutes later, when the hot iron touched the flesh to seal it, Neil squealed like a slaughtered animal, and so did Herb.

It was heart-wrenching.

Feeling sick, Karl thought he might have to go outside for fresh air. But he swallowed hard and held his ground and continued to help Isaacs. He and Isaacs checked for bleeding following the removal of the tourniquets above the knees. All was well.

"These two amputations have been successful. The arms will come off tomorrow," Isaacs was matter of fact as he handed Karl the makeshift surgical tools. He felt confident Neil would survive.

As Karl stood and looked at Neil Dewar, he wondered about his past and thought of his future. Living a life without legs or arms would not be easy. Neil would likely end up in some institution in England for the rest of his life. But what else could they have done? They had to do what they could to save his life.

In a short while, Neil started moving his head from side to side. Then he tried to sit up. He opened his eyes and stared at Karl who was standing next to him with a hand on one of his shoulders.

"My God, Karl, I'm still alive but I'm dying," he said several times.

"You are alive and you're going to be fine. The operation was successful," said Karl.

"Could you give me a drink of water?"

"No water for at least a couple of hours, but we can sponge your lips with a damp cloth," Isaacs spoke up. " We have to make sure bleeding doesn't start."

"Will I live another day, Mr. Isaacs?" Neil asked.

"You'll live to be an old man, probably outlive all of us," Isaacs smiled at him.

Neil stared at the two men and said, "The pain in my feet is gone. I don't know why."

Isaacs and Karl said nothing. It was Christmas Day. Hopefully, they had given Neil the gift of survival.

Chapter 21

DECEMBER 26

It was after twelve noon when Isaacs used the poker-hook to remove the iron bake-pot from the fireplace. He put the pot on the cooking stove to boil it and took off the cover to let the aroma circulate through the house.

"What a beautiful smell," Herb sniffed appreciatively. "Caribou meat must be the best meat in the world. We'll have to put a pastry over it, Mr. Isaacs. Makes the feast better."

Isaacs agreed and nominated Herb as the one to do it. Isaacs depended on Herb and felt bad that he'd had to pressure him to help with the amputations.

Herb washed his hands and rolled up his sleeves, he was familiar with cooking, especially mixing breads and pastry. Vegetables were in limited supply in the Pigeon, so Isaacs had made sure he had saved enough for Christmas Day dinner, especially potatoes and turnips.

Sam and George came to the House in time for dinner. They were not surprised to learn McFie had died. In fact, Sam was surprised to find Neil still living.

After the dinner feast was over and everything cleaned up, Isaacs asked Neil if he would like a drink of water and a little food. Neil refused the food but accepted the water.

"By supper time you should be feeling much better, you can eat then," he told Neil.

"I hope so, sir," said Neil.

"Your legs will start to heal very quickly because we removed all the infected parts. The greatest problem now is your hands. They are rotting hourly and getting worse and worse, especially the fingers. I'll be giving them a closer examination tonight," said Isaacs.

"I am very hungry. The smell of cooking meat is a torture. I would appreciate a large piece when the time comes," said Neil.

"Five o'clock, we'll give you supper," said Isaacs.

During the afternoon, Isaacs sang several old Christmas carols, but no one really listened. Karl fed Neil his supper, it wasn't a lot, just enough to satisfy him for a few hours. However, hot tea was what he craved.

Neil was taken from the bedroom where the operation had taken place and put back in his bunk. He was complaining about pain in his hands. Isaacs examined his hands and thought them much worse than in the morning.

"There is no doubt about it, Neil, blood poisoning has set in," he said. "If I had a brighter light, I would remove your hands tonight. But I don't so we will do it at first light tomorrow morning."

Neil didn't reply as he turned his face to the wall.

* * * * *

The morning of the 26th of December was a very cold one in L'Anse au Pigeon.

"The northwest wind is blowing its breath in the sun's face this morning, Skipper," said Karl after he came inside. "It's going to be a blustery day. There's two sun hounds peeking over the barrens, that calls for wind."

Isaacs was out of bed hours before daylight, his thoughts were on the job ahead. How successful would he be in removing

Neil's hands? They were poisonous well above the wrist and would have to be cut off halfway between the elbow and the wrist, or certainly above the infected part. He told Karl they would follow the same procedure they'd used on the feet with the hands in order to control the flow of blood.

"Is it necessary to use the hot iron? It wouldn't be as painful if you didn't use it," said Karl.

"The method we used in removing the legs was successful. I say we should do exactly the same thing to remove the arms," said Isaacs.

Herb concluded he would not be able to assist them.

"I have come to the end of my rope, my nerves will never stand another day hearing Neil screaming. Get Sam to help. Keep him here overnight and make him help you in the morning," he said.

"No. As soon as Sam is finished supper he is returning to Grandmother's Cove. We don't have the room for extra people. I need you, Herb, you know what to do," said Isaacs.

* * * * *

It was a clear cold morning, the sun was spreading its bright rays through the valleys of Quirpon Island and the ocean was perfectly still.

Isaac Isaacs had been awake for hours thinking about what he would have to do as soon as it got light enough. He had hoped he could remove one of Neil's arms today and another tomorrow or perhaps a few days from now. This would give him time to recuperate. However, both of Neil's hands were so infected it was dangerous to wait for another day.

Isaacs and Karl ate breakfast by lamplight. Herb was still in his bunk. He had twisted and turned all night.

"It's time you got out of the bunk, Herb," said Karl.

Herb threw back his heavy blanket, he was fully dressed, the only thing missing were his boots.

"It's a good morning for duck hunting, we should forget everything and launch a punt, we could even put out seal nets today," Herb said after he'd gone outside for a minute.

"No duck hunting today, Herb, maybe tomorrow," said Isaacs.

Herb walked to the table, picked up a mug and filled it with tea then he sat down.

"Looks like you fellows have had your breakfast."

"Yes, we are ready to go to work when you are," said Isaacs.

Herb was not happy, he wasn't sure if he should have breakfast or take a long walk.

"We had porridge and bread," said Karl.

"I'll have the same," said Herb. "How does Neil feel this morning, Skipper?"

"I haven't talked to him yet. But he slept well last night," Isaacs looked at Herb. "After you finish breakfast we will begin."

Herb didn't comment as he went about the business of eating his breakfast.

Neil lay in his bunk covered in dark blankets. The straw mattress he was on was soft and comfortable. It was like heaven compared to the ordeal he had gone through between the shipwreck and L'Anse au Pigeon. But the pain, the dreadful pain in his hands was now driving him crazy. His feet were gone. That pain had stopped, except for the burning in the area where they had been amputated.

Isaacs came over and asked him how he felt. Neil said he was hardly able to stand the pain in his hands.

"Do you have much pain in your legs?" Isaacs asked.

"Not much, only in the area where you took them off. And the pain in my groin is gone."

"That's good," said Isaacs. "Within a few days your legs will be pain free, it won't take long for them to heal."

"Are you going to remove my hands this morning?" Neil asked.

"Yes, we are. As soon as you are ready, we will relieve you of the infected hands that are causing you such pain."

"Are you sure my hands won't get better, sir? Are you sure they really have to come off?"

"I am going to take the bandages off and show them to you and let you make up your own mind. I think if you don't have them removed you are sure to die of blood poisoning, and that's something I know of no cure for."

Neil knew Isaacs was right. He was well aware his hands were getting worse; most of the flesh had already rotted and fallen off.

Although the sun was peeking over the horizon, it was not yet light enough to preform the operation. Isaacs lifted the lamp and held it close to Neil's face. He could see the anguish in his eyes, fear was written all over his face.

He placed the lamp on the stool and proceeded to take the bandages from his hands.

Neil winced in pain as Isaacs removed the bandages, taking strips of flesh with them. Most of the skin on the backs of his hands and around his fingers was gone; there was also a terrible stench!

"I will give you five minutes to decide what you're going to do. Let me know then or I'll decide for you," said Isaacs.

Neil couldn't stand the thought of having to go through another ordeal like the day before. One day in hell was enough. He wasn't sure if he was going to be able to endure another operation. But he concluded if he didn't have the operation he would die anyway. Perhaps even a more horrible death. Neil told Isaacs he would have the operation. But, he said, he wanted Herb to stand close by him as before. Both Isaacs and Herb agreed.

Isaacs had all the crude instruments ready, sterilized and placed on the chart table in the bedroom.

Karl, Herb and Matthew carried Neil into the room and placed him on the chart table. Isaacs took a wet soapy cloth and washed the area between the forearm and the elbow.

The three men put ropes around Neil and secured him on the table. It was too late now for him to change his mind, the operation would proceed.

His left arm was fastened tightly; the right one would come off first. Neil lay quietly with his eyes closed as if waiting for a knife to enter his flesh.

Karl gripped his arm, slightly above the wrist and pressed it down across the wooden block. Isaacs tightened the tourniquet above the elbow. Neil cringed with pain! Isaacs said his arm was all skin, muscle and sinew, and there wasn't much flesh to cut. He said the bones would be the biggest problem. He told Karl it was very important for him to hold the arm as securely as possible.

Isaacs pulled the blanket over Neil's upper body and gave Herb the signal to put the wooden pin in his mouth. Herb told Neil to bite hard on the pin.

Isaacs held the sharp pointed fish knife he had made as sharp as a razor and ready to go into action. The hacksaw lay on the table nearby.

Karl held the arm with his right hand, he knew it would not be secure enough when Isaacs started cutting. He would have to hold Neil's hand with his left. Because the hand was so tender, Neil would scream at the slightest touch, but it had to be done. Isaacs lifted the arm as Karl moved the block of wood to get it in an ideal position.

Isaacs nodded for Karl to take hold of the hand and hold it tightly. It was then the sharp fish knife did its work.

Isaacs cut the part toward the table first. Blood shot out on the surface. He severed the blood vessels and the ligaments. He cut each side and across the top, he cut keenly around the bones.

"Hold the hand steady, Karl, while I pull the flesh up over the bones and get ready to give me the saw."

Isaacs took the saw from Karl and drew it across the arm bone closest to his fingers, it took just three double strokes to sever the ulna, one of the two long bones in the forearm.

As Isaacs dug the teeth into the second bone, Neil let out a horrific scream and his body heaved up off the table.

"Hold the arm steady, Karl, for God's sake don't let it move around, it may splinter the bone," Isaacs roared.

Karl shifted his right hand closer to the saw and gripped the arm tighter. It was almost severed.

Isaacs made another push as the rest of the bone snapped and fell away.

"It's off, thank God, it's off," he said.

Karl saw a sharp piece of bone where it had broken but said nothing. He was relieved the arm was off.

Karl put the severed arm near the end of the table and reached for the line to use as a tourniquet, it was quickly applied near the end of the stump. Then he passed Isaacs the hot iron.

As Karl held the arm stump, Isaacs put the red hot iron on the raw flesh, it caused smoke when it touched and stuck to the skin. Isaacs wiggled the end and pulled it free. Then he dabbed it on several more times burning the surface again. Neil tried to pull what was left of his arm away but couldn't. Karl's grip was too firm. Neil screamed.

"Hold him steady, boys, we have to complete the job we started, it will soon be over." Isaacs bandaged the arm and put a loop of rope around it to keep it from moving while he severed the other one.

They had to move the chart table out from the wall in order to work on the other arm. Isaacs and Karl got in place.

"Good God, Mr. Isaacs, are you going to remove the other arm right away? You will kill him. You should wait a while," said Herb.

Isaacs appeared not to have heard him, he immediately started getting the tourniquet ready to apply above the elbow. Karl felt sick to his stomach. He wasn't sure if he could take another episode of stress and tension so soon.

"Are you losing your nerve, Karl, do you want to lie down?" asked Isaacs.

"I would like a breath of fresh air, sir."

"We have to finish the job first. Try and hold on a few more minutes." Isaacs sounded annoyed.

Karl took a deep breath and began to help his boss get ready to amputate the right arm. Herb then advised Isaacs he had to go outside for some fresh air. That put a halt to the proceedings. Herb had to be there to hold Neil's upper body. When Herb returned, Isaacs noticed Neil was fully conscious. His forehead was wet, but whether it was perspiration or water Herb had spilled on him he didn't know.

"Are you finished yet, Mr. Isaacs?" Neil asked.

"Very soon now."

The right arm was swollen more than the left, the infection was greater. Karl held the arm while Isaacs applied the tourniquet above the elbow, he pulled it very tight and tied it. Neil groaned. The slightest touch hurt his arm.

Herb put the wooden pin in Neil's mouth and held him down. Isaacs said not to let him move. Karl held the arm above the wrist with his left hand and caught hold of the infected hand with his right. Neil roared in pain.

Isaacs inserted the pointed knife into the back of the arm between the arm bones all the way through to the front. After letting the blood drain for a minute, he made an incision all the way around the arm. As Isaacs cut, he felt Neil's body tremble as if he would come off the table. Herb kept telling him to bite on the pin and said it would all be over in a few minutes. But the pain was too much for Neil. He blew the pin from his mouth and screamed.

"Don't let the hand get loose, hold it tight," Isaacs told Karl.

When the flesh was cut, most of the blood had run from the arm below the tourniquet. Isaacs pulled the flesh up toward the elbow, revealing the arm bones. He reached for the saw and quickly sawed the two arm bones off.

"No more infected hands," Isaacs commented.

Karl put the severed hand near the end of the table and helped Isaacs apply the tourniquet around the stump. When the tourniquet was applied Karl went to the fireplace and returned with the hot iron. Isaacs did the same as before, burned the stump-end to a crust. As he did so, Neil screamed to the high heavens.

"The job is completed, no more rotting feet or hands." Isaacs was exhausted.

Neil was silent as Isaacs bandaged the arm. The swollen area worried Isaacs, he knew it was caused by infection. He didn't know how far it had gone up his arm, he would have to pay special attention to it.

"That's fine, Herb," he said. "I can handle things from here, you can go."

Herb was happy it was over, and especially pleased that Neil would likely be okay. Isaacs removed the two tourniquets from above the elbows, relieved to see there wasn't any bleeding around the stumps.

"You will live to see dear old England again," Karl said as he leaned over to speak to Neil.

Karl couldn't help thinking that if Isaacs had operated on McFie the way he did on Neil, the sailor might still be alive.

Neil heard Karl's words through a fog of pain.

At the moment, he wasn't at all worried about whether or not he would ever see the shores of dear old England again.

His only concern was trying to battle the horrible pain that gripped his body.

It was now noon on December 26, 1816.

Chapter 22
SAVING NEIL'S LIFE

Neil was taken from the bedroom that had become the operating room. He was barely conscious. He was still shaking from the ordeal, but his breathing was stable. He was placed in his bunk near the fireplace and Isaacs wrapped him in a heavy dark blanket.

"We'll be very quiet, making sure not to disturb him. Right now sleep is the best medicine for him. After he wakes he should feel much better," said Isaacs.

Karl was doubtful, he couldn't understand how a little sleep could make a man feel better, especially after having his two hands and feet removed.

Shortly after getting Neil settled away, Isaacs and his men sat silently at the table eating lunch.

"It seems the sea has gone back," Isaacs said after a while. "If that's the case, we can launch a boat and put out the seal nets. The dog food is getting low. We'll need twenty or thirty carcasses to get the dogs through the winter. We'll need the same amount of skins... from old hoods (large migratory seals) if we can get them... for making boots."

"It's a bit early for old hoods," said Herb.

"The heavy ice will be coming south any day now and that usually brings a herd of old hoods before the harp seals come to pup further south," said Isaacs.

Herb nodded in agreement. Isaacs then turned to Karl.

"After we have lunch, Karl, you should go to the store-room and light a fire to warm the place up. We'll go down there and have a talk about what we should do."

"We've got the fire going now, sir," said Matthew.

"That's fine. Alright then, Karl, you stay here and watch Neil, clean the dishes and tidy the place up," said Isaacs.

"Yes sir," Karl replied.

Neil slept for most of the afternoon, groaning and twitching in his sleep. Karl sat near the table and watched him. At around four o'clock, Isaacs crept into the house and asked how Neil was doing.

"He is still sleeping, moved a few times but didn't wake. His breathing seems fine," said Karl.

"It's going to take twenty-four hours before we know what's going to happen. After a couple of days he will be out of danger of blood clots," said Isaacs.

"He has had a hard time," Karl looked with sympathy at the man lying on the bunk. "It's amazing he's still alive, he must have been a tough man. It would be too bad to lose him now."

"You've got no worries there. He'll probably outlive you and I," Isaacs patted Karl's shoulder.

"I hope you're right," said Karl.

Who was going to look after Neil? Karl wanted to know. Whose job would it be to help Neil with things like using the bathroom? Isaacs said it would probably be him and Karl.

Isaacs was all too well aware that everything in life was going to be hard, if not impossible, for a man with no hands. That was not anything to worry about now, however.

Saving Neil's life was their immediate priority.

Chapter 23

MOVING TO THE WINTER CAMP

The afternoon dragged on. At four thirty, Isaacs asked Karl to light the lamps. He also asked Herb to make a pot of soup, something that would be good for Neil to eat when he woke up.

Shortly before six, Neil opened his eyes. He called Karl who went to his bunk and asked him what he wanted. Neil said he had a terrible headache and would like a drink of water. Karl asked Isaacs if Neil was allowed to have water. Isaacs said just a little so Karl gave him some and raised his pillow higher. Isaacs put a vinegar soaked cloth on Neil's forehead, saying it was good for curing headaches. He asked Neil how he felt other than the headache.

Neil thought for a moment then replied jokingly, "I don't have any pain in my hands or feet. It's the same as if I didn't have them. And my headache is getting better."

"You're going to be all right, Neil. Give you a month and your operation should be all healed. You'll be out on the move then," Herb came over to stand by his bunk.

Neil had a feeling he would be okay. The burning that had tortured him for a whole month was gone. He was still having pain. But it was easier to bear than the burning.

Herb served him up a small bowl of vegetables and meat from the soup. Isaccs said he had to wait until the next day before he could have liquids.

Herb found it difficult to look at Neil. It wasn't easy to see a man who had been six feet tall and now was reduced to four and a half feet.

After Neil had eaten his supper, Isaacs decided to examine his legs and if possible remove the tourniquets. There was a lot of swelling between the knees and the site of the amputation. Isaacs figured this was caused by the tourniquets so he removed them. There was a little bleeding but nothing to be alarmed about. He applied a coating of turpentine and decided to leave the wounds open for a few hours before applying more. He then wrapped Neil in a heavy blanket and told him to try to get as much sleep as possible.

Neil slept for most of the night.

Shortly before daylight, Isaacs arose from his bed and lit the lamp. He knew a storm was brewing; the wind was picking up from the northeast or southeast. He made his usual early morning trip outside. When he returned he announced that the sea was beginning to heave. It was also very cold out.

"We won't get much done today," he said. "We're in for a heavy fall of snow. We are also going to have drifting snow. It's beginning now."

John and Matthew were sitting near the fireplace; they had kept the fire going all night. When Neil saw Isaacs come inside, he asked for a mug of water.

"How are you feeling this morning, Neil?" Isaacs asked.

"Very good, sir. Still got a lot of pain but I feel much better."

"I'm glad to hear that. Makes the storm outside somewhat unimportant." Isaacs got Neil a mug half full of water. "Once it's light enough, I am going to dress your wounds. What we have to do now is avoid infection the very best we can. If we can do that it won't take long for you to heal."

Karl suggested Herb put on a pot of rolled oats for breakfast, saying it would make a nice change from salt fish. Herb got up, took soap and towel and went outside.

"One thing with Herb," Karl grinned. "He doesn't need water to wash himself, all he needs is lots of snow and soap. I always say he has shark's skin."

"Everyone should be like that, save a lot of fooling around," said Isaacs.

"Not me, I'm not made that way," said Karl.

Isaacs asked Karl if he'd heard the dogs barking in the night. Karl said he hadn't.

"I heard them," Neil spoke quickly.

"So you heard them too," Isaacs nodded. "They were barking for about ten minutes. Something must have been around, they must have heard something."

"Maybe it was a polar bear," said Karl. "The northern slob ice should be getting close to this area. I thought I saw it from the hill yesterday. It looked like a white cast on the horizon far off to the east. Usually, when it arrives, there'll be a polar bear or two with it. Maybe that was what the dogs were barking at last night."

"I heard the sea this morning. That shows the heavy northern slob isn't close to the shore yet," Isaacs said after a minute's thought.

"Maybe a company of shore ducks was feeding in the harbour," said Herb. "Several thousand ducks make a lot of noise. That could have been what the dogs were barking at."

"After daylight I'm going to take a musket and have a look around. Might get a shot at the shore ducks if they're around. It would be great if we had a few for the pot," said Karl.

Herb finished cooking the pot of rolled oats. Karl asked Neil if he was ready to have his breakfast and he said he was.

"Well, come on to the table then, what's keeping you?" Karl grinned at him.

"Don't worry, Karl, I'll be coming to the table sooner than you think," Neil grinned back.

Isaacs was happy to hear Neil sounding so positive.

Karl fed Neil a bowl of porridge and a slice of bread and that was very encouraging for everyone.

After breakfast was eaten and everything cleaned and put away, Isaacs told the men to get back to their normal duties. He said he would take care of Neil and do the housework. Everybody was more than happy to hear that, especially Herb, who usually did most of the cooking. Herb was eager to get out around the headlands with his gun.

"This afternoon, Sam and I are going to harness the dogs and go to Grandmother's Cove," said Karl. "There may be seals up on the ice in the harbour. We may kill a few, if we're lucky."

"Good idea," said Isaacs. "If you get one, bring back some of the meat. I'll fry it for supper, a good meal of fresh seal meat would be a treat."

After everyone had left, Isaacs decided to examine Neil's wounds. He wanted to keep an eye out for any signs of infection. Everything looked fine, but there was considerable swelling around the upper legs. He considered that normal, taking into account the bones that had been severed.

"In a couple of days you should be pain free and the healing will begin," he told Neil.

"I don't have a lot of pain now, sir. Nothing like the burning I suffered in my feet and hands," said Neil.

"That is almost as big a relief to me as it is to you. When you suffer we all suffer."

"What do you think will happen to me now, Mr. Isaacs?" asked Neil.

Isaacs thought for a minute, he knew what Neil had on his mind. "I think it's too early for you to be thinking about that," he said finally.

"I'm going to have to start thinking about how I am going to get around, especially here at the house," said Neil. "I don't have feet to walk any more, I don't have hands to feed myself or make a living. What will I do?"

Isaacs knew there was very little he could say. Neil was talking about reality, but it was too early to face it yet.

"I'll tell you what," said Isaacs, "after your legs and arms heal, we will begin making plans to help you become independent. There are certain things we can do."

Neil dropped the subject. He knew his first concern was trying to stay alive and get well. He was determined that if he recovered from this ordeal, he was not going to stay in the bunk all day, begging, no matter what it took.

Isaacs treated Neil with the best care he could possibly give him, using the limited home remedies he thought would help him heal.

As Isaacs tended to Neil, Karl and Herb harvested several seals around the edge of the ice near Quirpon Harbour. They also killed many shore ducks the week after Christmas. The men had a dinner feast every evening: seal, duck and caribou. Usually the meat was covered with pastry and baked in the oven.

Three days after the amputations, Neil was sitting at the table and being fed by Karl. He didn't mind being fed. His greatest embarrassment was being cleaned after answering nature's call. His amputations were very sore and tender but even though they were slow to heal, they showed good progress.

"We have to move to our winter camp next week," Isaacs told Neil one day. "You should be able to travel by then. Herb will be staying here to look after the place."

Herb knew what his duties were. When everyone was gone, he would spend his time mending nets. This was part of the contract with the French Captains. He would also make bread for the crew working in the woods at the green ridge, South West Arm.

Isaacs said the ice on Quirpon Harbour should be strong enough to cross on after New Year's Day and so the packing began.

"We'll have to make several trips to get everything taken to the hut," said Karl. "We won't be able to take very much on the first trip. We'll have to beat a track; a lot of snow fell during the last few days."

"I'm surprised Sam hasn't been here. Guess we can expect him any day," said Herb.

"I told him to wait till the ice in the harbour was safe enough to cross over. Maybe that's what he's waiting for," said Isaacs.

"We've had a lot of frost last week, it should be okay now," said Karl.

"I guess he doesn't want anyone to end up in the water. Sam is very careful," said Isaacs.

During the afternoon, Sam arrived and announced that the ice in the harbour was safe enough to cross on.

The party prepared to move to the heavily wooded area that was eight miles away.

Chapter 24
GETTING SETTLED

It took the men three days to move the supplies and material to the winter hut at South West Arm. They were ten miles from the Indian tilt where Neil and his two companions first met Joseph, the Indian who took them in and gave them directions to Isaacs on Quirpon Island.

The first Monday after New Year's Day, Isaacs placed Neil in a sleigh pulled by a team of twelve dogs. Neil's wounds were heavily wrapped in blankets and he sat on a straw mattress with pillows to rest his legs on. The driver was Karl. Isaacs stood at the rear and kept a close eye on Neil.

It was a rough ride. During the trip, Neil was tossed about mercilessly. Although his wounds were well covered they were far from healed and his left arm became infected when the fishing line was removed from the cut-off area.

It was discovered that when Isaacs burned the area with the hot iron, he had slightly burned the line, and the ash from it could have caused the infection.

Isaacs took a sterilized knife and cut away the infected tissue. This was very unpleasant for Neil. However, he had no choice but to endure it. The infection cleared up after a few days.

* * * * *

Their new home was a log hut measuring six feet high on the sides and eight feet in the peak. It was built from logs standing on end and the seams were filled with moss. The hut was twenty feet long by fourteen feet wide, with a large fireplace at the end, used for heat and cooking.

Twenty feet away was another building, this was where Sam stayed with the Indians. Neil, Karl and Isaacs stayed in the larger tilt.

Isaacs had work planned for the men. They were to cut and saw logs enough to build another room onto the house at The Pigeon and a shed near the wharf. They would use a pit saw for sawing lumber and cut trees with an axe and cross-cut saw.

When Isaacs and the crew arrived at the hut it was completely covered in snow. The only sign of a building was the flagpole going up on the side near the chimney.

The men dug the snow away from the roof until they found the doorway and made steps to get down into it. Karl then dug out the windows to allow light inside.

"Be careful you don't break the windows with the shovel," Isaacs warned Karl.

After the tunnel was dug and snow cleared from the entrance Neil was carried down into the hut. He was surprised to see such a comfortable place. Sam lit the fireplace, and in a few minutes the hut was cosy and warm.

Neil was put in a bunk near the fireplace and close to the table. Isaacs said he could sleep in the bunk and use it as a seat when he sat at the table.

The men brought most of the food supplies into the hut, the remainder was taken to the shed nearby. The dogs' house was also dug out and made ready.

"Herb will be baking bread for us back at The Pigeon. We will use an average of four loaves a day. Once a week, we have to go in with a load of lumber and that's when we'll bring back the bread," said Isaacs. He added that would be Karl's job as he was handy with the dogs.

"This will be a very busy place for the next two months," Isaacs continued. "We have to cut enough firewood for the two houses for at least one full year, maybe more. Then the wood will be put out to the shoreline, to be taken to The Pigeon by boat next spring, as soon as the ice is gone. John and George and Matthew will be going hunting and trapping. We need caribou. It's the best meat there is, and caribou hides make good boots."

"The caribou herd should be close to here. They're probably on the White Hills or on the eastern bogs," said Karl.

The Indians were happy to hear they were going hunting and trapping; they would be gone for at least a week at a time. Sam, Karl, and Isaacs would be cutting logs and sawing lumber for the first month. After that, they would be cutting firewood and hauling it out to the beach, and stacking it near the high water mark.

During the long winter nights, everyone would be busy making skin boots and parkas. Isaacs had requests from the French Admirals for two hundred pairs of boots and unlimited numbers of parkas, all made from seal skins.

They usually began making them March 1st, using skins they had tanned during the previous summer. The Indians were experts at making skin boot and coats.

* * * * *

It was late afternoon when the crew got settled away.

"It's better for you to stay here with us in the big hut because the Indians will be gone hunting most of the time." Isaacs told Sam.

Sam was happy to stay in the big hut, But he knew when Joseph arrived from Pistolet Bay, he would have to move.

Chapter 25
BACK TO THE PIGEON

After Isaacs had everyone settled away he sent for Joseph, the Indian trapper at Pistolet Bay. He was anxious to know if he had done well with the furs: muskrat and beaver. He needed them to use as trimmings for the seal skin parkas he would make for the French Admirals.

Neil was eager to see Joseph again. He wanted to thank him for the directions he'd provided that had saved his life.

In chats with Joseph, Neil was surprised to learn that he and the other Indians came from Chateau Bay, Labrador, although they said their parents were born on Quirpon Island.

Joseph was actually named after famed English naturalist and explorer Sir Joseph Banks. His parents had met Banks many times while he was at Quirpon in the late 1700s. Banks came to Newfoundland to study its natural history in 1766, and returned to England a year later with descriptions of numerous plants and animals. He brought back 340 plants and documented 34 species of birds, including the Great Auk.

As time advanced, Neil became stronger. His wounds healed as well as expected except for his left leg which caused him a problem. If he touched his left leg against anything it felt as though a knife was sticking in his flesh. He didn't know it, but the problem was a sharp edge of bone which had splintered while Isaacs was sawing and was now keeping the wound open.

Every night Isaacs would bathe Neil's wounds in hot salted water. Afterwards, he would apply castor oil and turpentine. When Neil's left leg became infected, Isaacs suspected it was caused by the saw not being sufficiently sterilized when he was performing the amputation.

"It appears the end of the leg bone is infected," he told Neil. "In order to get rid of the infection, I may have to saw the bones off again, maybe take off three or four inches more."

Neil was devastated by his words.

"I think I would rather die, Mr. Isaacs, than go through another operation. I wouldn't be able to bear it."

"I will give it another forty-eight hours. If there isn't an improvement by then, something will have to be done," said Isaacs

The thought of having to hold Neil down while Isaacs sawed off the bones in his leg again horrified Karl.

"Mr. Isaacs," he suggested, "why don't you boil cod liver oil and make a cod liver oil poultice. That might draw out the infection. My mother swore by cod liver oil poultices."

Isaacs was a man willing to listen to anyone prepared to talk sense. He said the idea was worth trying. The only thing was that their supply of cod liver oil was back at The Pigeon. Karl said he would go back and get it the next day.

"It's a great night," said Isaacs. "Maybe you and Sam should go now, there's a track all the way. And when you come back you can bring along whatever bread Herb has baked for us."

"We are going to need more seal oil for the lamps too," said Karl. "Did the Indians render out any seal fat?"

"Yes, I think they did. I smelled an awful stench down in the stage when I was at The Pigeon last week. Check on it. If it's there bring back five gallons."

When Karl and Sam returned with the cod liver oil and the seal oil and four loaves of bread, Isaacs made a cod liver oil poultice. It helped, but didn't cure, Neil's infected leg. Even though the leg was still infected, Neil was experiencing a pain-free body. Isaacs, however, still wanted to cure the leg.

The long nights at the hut made for a lot of stories as the men worked at making seal skin boots and coats. Neil had to tell them about his experience cruising the Spanish Main and the coast of Africa while in the Royal Navy. Isaacs had to relate his naval experiences. By the time April rolled around, most everyone had revealed their life history and a few secrets.

Neil's wounds healed – Isaacs referred to them as being skinned over. Isaacs hollowed out pieces of wood that strapped to Neil's arm stumps. He had places where eating utensils or a quill pen could be inserted into the wood. After weeks of practice, Neil was able to feed himself and had made a start at writing.

Isaacs made caribou skin pads, padded them with hair from the hides and put them on Neil's leg stumps. One leg could bear his weight, the left leg was still sore.

With the help of an empty flour barrel placed under his chest, Neil was able to roll around inside and outside the hut. The ideas that Isaacs came up with amazed Neil and the rest of the men.

Spring finally rolled around and the party moved back to the house at The Pigeon. Isaacs had had a very successful winter in the country. It was time now to go hunting seals.

Chapter 26

FAREWELL

During the first week in May most of the snow had melted. As the ground began to thaw, Neil was anxious to know when his two friends who had died would be buried.

"Mr. Isaacs, when do you intend to bury Donaldson and McFie? The ground should be thawed enough by now. I want to make sure they have a Christian burial," he said.

"Neil, I forgot to tell you. The boys buried them last week. They were forced too, due to the stench up in the loft. They dug a very deep grave on one of the islands and Herb gave them a decent burial. He knows as much about that as I do," Isaacs lied.

The fact was that after the ice moved and the men got the boat in the water to start seal hunting, Isaacs told Herb and Karl to give the two men a burial at sea. They did that approximately half a mile off The Pigeon.

* * * * *

As the last week of May rolled around and navigation opened up, Isaacs launched his boats and prepared to move to his summer fishing quarters at Clue Cove, two miles west of The Pigeon. Here he would fish for salmon, arctic char and sea trout. The French would buy his total catch and supply the barrels and salt to cure it all. The French themselves fished for cod only.

Around the first week in June, the first French fishing vessels arrived. They were a welcome sight for Isaacs and his men. The arriving ships had fresh supplies, some vessels even carried a cow or two. Isaacs and his men looked forward to fresh milk, the most welcome treat of all.

After the fishing premises were inspected and everything was deemed acceptable, Isaacs and his men got paid for their duties, first in food and supplies, the remainder in English currency.

The skin products they'd made during the winter... moccasins, boots, coats and gloves... were sold and paid for with cash. Neil was very impressed with the business dealings between Isaacs and the French.

The French Captains had received word to be on the lookout for the vessel *Rebecca* that was missing without a trace. They were surprised to learn of its fate and most of the French fishermen walked to Clue Cove to see Neil and listen to what they could understand of his story.

The French vessels would not be returning to France till after the fishing season, probably in late September. A report about Neil and the *Rebecca* would not reach Europe until they returned, unless another ship visited.

* * * * *

During the month of July, the amputated areas on Neil's legs became sore and infection set in, perhaps caused by his moving around too much on his stumps.

Isaacs told him to stay off his stumps until they healed.

Neil found that hard to do. He was enjoying his freedom in the cabin and around the outside at Clue Cove. It was such a beautiful place. Isaacs kept a close eye on Neil, staying within talking distance of him most of the time.

Isaacs left word with the French that if a vessel came to The

Pigeon going anywhere there was a hospital to make sure to notify him... or have it come to Clue Cove and pick up Neil.

The French fishing vessels were gearing up to return to St. Malo, France, with a full load of dried cod the last week of August. Neil was scheduled to return to Europe with them. Neil's legs were in bad condition and appeared to be getting worse and Isaacs could not cure the infection.

A day before the fishing vessels departed The Pigeon, the French supply vessel arrived.

The *Lilly* of Quebec had all of Isaacs' winter supplies aboard. Captain Stewart said when the *Lilly* left The Pigeon it was proceeding on to Montreal, Quebec.

Word was sent to Isaacs to come to The Pigeon and supervise the unloading of his winter supplies. Captain Stewart asked Isaacs if he had heard or seen anything of a missing vessel named the *Rebecca*.

"The ship has been missing since last November. It disappeared without a trace. It was last seen near Cape Charles, Labrador," he said.

"We know all about the *Rebecca* and its disappearance," said Isaacs.

He went on to tell Captain Stewart the whole story about Neil Dewar and plotted on his chart where the *Rebecca* went on the rocks.

"Neil is with us at our cabin in Clue Cove. He has infected legs from where we had to amputate his feet in order to save his life. He needs to get to a hospital as soon as possible or I fear the worst," said Isaacs.

"I am on my way to Montreal and I am quite willing to give him passage," said Captain Stewart. "We will come to Clue Cove and pick him up this evening."

Isaacs was overjoyed by the offer. He hurried back to Clue Cove and proceeded to get Neil ready for the trip to Montreal.

He called his men together and told them Neil was leaving within the hour.

Karl felt sad about Neil leaving. They had become close friends during the months Karl had tended him day and night.

"I will miss you, Karl," Neil had tears in his eyes as he bid his friend farewell. "I don't know how I will make it without you. I don't know how I am going to ask someone else to do all of the things you have done for me."

"If your leg stumps were not infected there would be no need for you to leave... you can't do anything more in England than you can here. We would like you to stay here with us, you're part of our family," Karl spoke from his heart.

"He needs special medical attention that we can't give him here," Isaacs broke in. "The *Lilly* has medical supplies aboard and someone who knows how to use it. Neil will be fine with Captain Stewart."

At three in the afternoon the *Lilly* anchored off Clue Cove and blew its horn.

It was time to leave.

Neil dreaded to say goodbye to the people who had saved his life. He loved each one of them.

Karl and Herb put him on a chair and carried him to the stage head. He looked out the harbour at the ship that would take him away forever. All of the other men stood around him and said a tearful goodbye. Neil hugged each one of them the best way he could and thanked them with all his heart for what they had done for him.

"I will never ever forget any of you. You treated me as though I was a member of your family. I will always be grateful to you," Neil couldn't stop his tears from falling.

Before he left to board the *Lilly* he put his arm stumps around Isaacs again.

"Thanks for what you did, Mr. Isaacs. I know it must have

broken your heart to cause me such pain while you were sawing off my arms and legs. But I know it took pain to save my life. I will never be able to repay you. If I ever get back home to England and if any of you are ever near the Isle of Wight, come and see me, you'll be more than welcome."

Isaacs promised him they would. He and Karl and Herb then brought Neil to the ship where he was welcomed aboard by Captain Stewart.

In just a few minutes Neil waved goodbye to Clue Cove and to the men who had saved his life.

Chapter 27

MR. CUMMINGS

The *Lilly* of Quebec headed westward up the Gulf of St. Lawrence. Captain Stewart was a good skipper and a very mild mannered man. He gave Neil his cabin and personally attended to his sore legs, dressing them daily. He cut pillows in two to make cushions for Neil's knees and brought him up on deck when the weather was favourable.

The trip took much longer than usual, at one place they were storm bound for a full week. When they finally arrived in Montreal, Neil was taken to a hospital and attended to by nuns.

After a close examination by Doctors Hicket and Holmes, it was determined the amputation done by Isaacs was not a very smooth job. The bones were left with very sharp edges. One bone was found to be only partly sawed then broken. This had caused the spear like edge to penetrate the flesh, preventing the wound from healing. There was also signs of bone infection.

The doctors decided to amputate the legs again.

During the operation, Neil did not suffer as he had at the house in L'Anse au Pigeon. He thanked God when he was given ether to put him to sleep.

Neil's legs were made four inches shorter. After the operation, the doctors were worried about bone infection. Neil was, however, given the best of care and started to improve.

As word started to spread about Neil Dewar and what had

happened to him and the ship *Rebecca*, families who had loved ones aboard wanted to know the whole story.

Neil told the story to anyone who wanted to hear it.

One day, Emily Cummings' father came to visit him.

Mr. Cummings, who had travelled all the way from his home in London, was in his mid-sixties. He was surprised to find that Neil was in his early twenties. He had assumed as an officer on the ship he would be much older.

"If you are up to it, young man, I want to know all the details about the voyage of the *Rebecca*, from the day it left to when it went on the rocks on the coast of Newfoundland," he said.

"I will try and tell you everything, although probably there are some things you may not want to hear." Neil spoke softly. "There are things I have tried to block out of my memory, things that haunt me everytime I close my eyes. I so wish I had taken control of the *Rebecca* when your daughter wanted me too. That is something I will regret forever."

"I want to hear everything that happened. I sent my daughter to England, not to Labrador, so please tell me everything you can so that I can understand," Mr. Cummings was begging.

Neil related every detail about the voyage and what went on aboard the *Rebecca*. He told about the shipwreck and about Emily coming on deck the last time he saw her.

He went on to tell him how Isaacs had to saw off his arms and legs in order to save his life, and how Donaldson and McFie had died in the process.

Everything was related to Mr. Cummings who sat stoney-faced and silent. Every so often he would stop Neil and take notes and wipe tears from his eyes. After Neil finished telling him the whole story, he put his face in his hands and wept.

"My wife and I loved our daughter deeply," he said as he finally raised his head and looked at Neil. "She was the only child we had. I wanted her to go back to London and finish school.

The owners of the vessel said it would be a safe voyage. No one said she had to go to Labrador for fish to take to Cadiz. If I had known about it, she would not have gone on that ship."

Mr. Cummings reached into his breast pocket and brought out a small oval frame in which there was a photograph of two remarkably similar women. The older woman was looking lovingly at the younger woman.

"That's Emily with her mother," he said as he showed the picture to Neil. "You can see how much alike they are."

"They are both beautiful," Neil held the picture and looked intently at it. There was a silence as both he and Mr. Cummings thought sadly about what could have been. What might have been.

Cummings broke the silence.

"Young man," he said, as he cleared his throat. "What do you intend to do when you go back to England?"

"I'm not sure yet, sir. These days if a sailor gets discharged from the Navy with good arms and legs, he can have a problem getting a job. With no arms or legs the problems increases dramatically. As for me, I will probably sit by the side of the highway, begging," Neil tried to grin.

The elderly gentleman reached into his pocket and this time he brought out a white linen handkerchief. He blew his nose long and noisily before speaking.

"Don't worry, son," he said. "You won't have to beg as long as I have a dollar."

"Thank you for saying that, sir," Neil looked into his eyes. "I should tell you that the man who sawed off my legs and arms taught me how to write by inserting a quill pen at the end of the hands he made me. He believed I could be whatever I wanted to be and I believe that too, sir. I am determined not to be a burden. I am determined to be the best I can be."

Cummings was pleased to hear this positive talk.

He took a notebook from his pants pocket, wrote in it and said, "I am going to put you on our payroll. When you get to London you can learn how to use artificial limbs. I too believe you can do anything you want to do."

Neil thanked him and gladly accepted his offer.

After two months in hospital, Neil returned to England where he had several more operations on his legs. He liked to say that he was likely the only man to ever have his legs amputated three times.

He went on to become a book-keeper and was pleased to accept a position offered by Mr. Cummings in his London office.

Although Neil's sailing days were over he never ever forgot the long days he and his companions spent searching for *The Place Called Quirpon.*

Acknowledgements

Special thanks to Iris Fillier and Alvine Sutton for helping with editing. Special thanks to Max Snook of Grand Bank for helping with the book and with editing.

Special thanks to: Bill Quinton Bartlett of Griquet, Nelson and Sharon Roberts of Quirpon; and to Frank Elliott, Nancy Pilgrim, Richard Kenney, Marsha Pilgrim, George Humby, and Caesar Pilgrim.

Special thanks to Harry Steele for encouraging me to write stories that should be written.

As always, special thanks to my wife Beatrice for her help and assistance.

Finally a special thanks to all my loyal readers.

About the Author

Earl B. Pilgrim, Newfoundland and Labrador's favourite storyteller, was born in Roddickton in 1939 and still lives there with his wife Beatrice. He and his wife have four grown children.

Earl started his working career in the Canadian Army where he got involved in the sport of boxing and went on to become Canadian Light Heavyweight Boxing Champion.

Following his stint in the Army, he worked as a Forest Ranger with the Newfoundland and Labrador Forestry Department. Nine years later he became a Wildlife Protection Officer with the Newfoundland Wildlife Division.

Earl has won many awards for his work, including the Queen Elizabeth II Golden Jubilee Medal; the Safari International Award; the Gunther Behr Award; and the Achievement Beyond the Call of Duty Award.

Earl and his son, Norman, have a wilderness lodge in the mountains of the Cloud River near Roddickton. They offer big game hunting for moose, caribou and black bear in the fall and snowmobiling in the winter. During summer, guests can fish for salmon or trout. The area where the lodge is located is one of the most successful on the island for all of these endeavours.

Earl can be reached by calling 709-457-2041, cell 709-457-7071 or e-mail earl.pilgrim@nf.sympatico.ca.

Web address is www.boughwiffenoutfitters.com

Other great reads from Earl by DRC Publishing:

The Day of Varick Frissell
The untold story of a daring young American film maker who was aboard the *SS Viking* the day she sailed to her doom from St. John's harbour.

The Sheppards are Coming
Read about the daring exploits of Brig Bay natives Kenneth Sheppard and his sons Tom and Carl as they defy the law on Prohibition in their schooner *Minnie Rose* – with success but not without consequences!

The Day Grenfell Cried
The true story of what happened when Dr. Wilfred Grenfell helped the poor people of northern Newfoundland and Labrador. Grenfell's compassion brought him into conflict with powerful fish merchants and almost broke his heart.

Marguerite of the Isle of Demons
An exciting true story of a French princess abandoned on a desolate island off northern Newfoundland in the 16th century. A moving fast paced story of survival against all odds by Newfoundland and Labrador's favourite storyteller.

Jump Ranger Jump
In May of 1943, Newfoundland Ranger Jack Hogan was one of four men who jumped from a burning airplane over the Northern Peninsula of Newfoundland. Hogan and RAF Corporal Eric Butt were the only survivors.

Drifting Into Doom
In January 1883, Howard Blackburn, a Nova Scotia native fishing out of Gloucester, Mass, and his dory mate, Thomas Welsh, a 16-year-old from Grand Bank, NL, went adrift from their schooner *Grace L. Fears* while fishing off the Burgeo Banks.

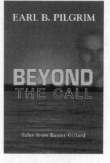

Beyond The Call
The tales of Doctor Baxter Gillard are true stories which will be enjoyed by everyone, especially those who love wilderness adventures.